Donal Ryan was born in a village in North Tipperary, a stroll from the shores of Lough Derg. He wrote the first draft of *The Spinning Heart*, his debut novel, in the long summer evenings of 2010. Never one to give up, Ryan received 47 rejections over three years before becoming a published author, and the rest — as they say — is history; *The Spinning Heart* was longlisted for the Man Booker Prize and was voted Book of the Year at the 2012 Irish Book Awards. His second novel, *The Thing About December*, confirms his status as one of the best writers of his generation. Ryan now lives in Limerick with his wife and children.

THE THING ABOUT DECEMBER

Johnsey is not quite like other people. He finds it hard to fit in, especially in a small Irish community. Regularly bullied, without friends, struggling to make sense of the world around him, he is particularly vulnerable when his parents die and he is left completely alone. He also owns land — land that has now become extremely valuable — and it seems that everyone around him wants to take advantage of his innocence and force him to sell. Village bullies and scheming land-grabbers stand in his way, no matter where he turns. Set over the course of one year of Johnsey's life, *The Thing About December* is a heart-twisting tale of a lonely man trying to make his way in a world moving faster than he is.

Books by Donal Ryan
Published by The House of Ulverscroft:

THE SPINNING HEART

DONAL RYAN

◆

THE THING ABOUT DECEMBER

Complete and Unabridged

CHARNWOOD
Leicester

First published in Great Britain in 2013 by
Doubleday Ireland
an imprint of
The Random House Group Limited
London

First Charnwood Edition
published 2014
by arrangement with
The Random House Group Limited
London

The lines from 'Memory of My Father' by Patrick Kavanagh are reprinted from *Collected Poems* edited by Antoinette Quinn (Allen Lane, 2004), by kind permission of the Trustees of the Estate of the late Katherine B. Kavanagh, through the Jonathan Williams Literary Agency.

A catalogue record for this book is available from the British Library.

ISBN 978-1-4448-2097-3

Published by
F. A. Thorpe (Publishing)
Anstey, Leicestershire

Set by Words & Graphics Ltd.
Anstey, Leicestershire
Printed and bound in Great Britain by
T. J. International Ltd., Padstow, Cornwall

This book is printed on acid-free paper

For Anne Marie, with love.

January

Mother always said January is a lovely month. Everything starts over again in the New Year. The visitors are all finished with and you won't see sight nor hear sound of them until next Christmas with the help of God. Before you know it you'll see a stretch in the evenings. The calving starts in January and as each new life wobbles into the slatted house your wealth grows a little bit. It'd want to — you have to try and claw back what was squandered in December on rubbish that no one really wanted. The bit of frost kills any lingering badness. That's the thing about January: it makes the world fresh. That's what Mother used to say anyway, back when she used to have a lot more to say for herself.

★ ★ ★

Eugene Penrose and his pals were sitting on the low wall in front of the IRA memorial again. Isn't it a fright to God to say a man can't walk home without being tormented by yahoos every single day? A few times lately Eugene had clipped Johnsey's heel as he walked past them and he had stumbled and nearly fallen. How could they be always there anyway? The dole is great, Mother says. It allows thugs to live like little lords. How's it he couldn't be a proper man, besides creeping along like a red-faced

1

child, afraid of his own shadow, with tears of shame stinging at his eyes? Daddy wouldn't have put up with it, that's for sure.

People used to be afraid of Johnsey's father. He'd give ground to no man. He loved a good row at the mart or at a match or above in the yard about the worth of a player or the price of a beast or anything you could imagine men might argue about. But he was as well known for his kindness as for his fury. His kindness was never taken for weakness, though: Daddy was a tough yoke. He'd shouldered many a big forward into the middle of next week in his days playing hurling; Johnsey had often heard that said or something like it. Once he had worn a hurley off of a lad in pure-solid temper and the same lad was never again right after it. Johnsey had only heard that said once, and when the man saying it saw that he was listening, he stopped talking and looked into his glass of whiskey and turned red.

★ ★ ★

If he thought about something else while he walked the hundred-odd steps from the start of the low wall to the far end of the churchyard he could nearly cod himself that they weren't there at all, watching him coming, looking forward to making little of him. Like the deep pool in the stream down past the weeping willow at the far end of the river field as you start towards the Shannon Callows where he and Daddy used to swim. Sometimes Johnsey wondered what would it be like to lie down under that water and, when all the breath in his lungs was gone, just stay down there and breathe in water instead of air. Maybe a miracle would happen like the ones that happened below in Cork years ago where the statue of the Virgin Mary came alive and said hello to everyone and cried blood over the state of the world. Mother said it was the state of the hairy mollies gawking up at her that made her cry. Wouldn't you cry too if you had that shower roaring the holy rosary up at you night and day? Maybe, instead of drowning, he'd discover he had superhuman powers, that he was able to live under the water and could control the streams and the rivers and the sea and all that lived there, and he could live there himself and be a king, with a deadly-sharp three-pronged fork, and loads of beautiful mermaids swimming around with no bras on and making him his dinner and kissing him.

Maybe when he gets home Mother will have a tart made for after the dinner, and she'll be just taking it out of the oven when he arrives. He'll eat a huge cut of it and she'll stand behind him with a mug of tea (just a tiny drop of milk, otherwise it's ruined, Mother says) and tell him how them apples were still growing outside not even an hour ago. He'll tell her it was a lovely dinner and she'll say Was it, pet, I hope it was, you need a good dinner after your hard day. These days, though, nearly always, she would have his dinner left in the oven and it would be blistering hot or freezing cold; she sometimes left the oven on too high or forgot to leave it on at all, and she herself would be above at the Height where Daddy was buried, saying prayers and cursing at the weeds. All the prayers she was saying for him, he must be getting no respite above in heaven. Father Cotter said at his Mass that there would be a fine house ready for him above and he'd probably start a fight with the angels over the design of it and want it knocked and built again to his own specifications. The neighbours all laughed at that. Some of them even looked at each other and smiled knowingly; sure he was a divil for exactness, you couldn't do a job right for him.

Mother wasn't home. There was a shepherd's pie in the oven, at a proper temperature, covered in tinfoil, and cutlery on the table. He ate it fast, and gulped a glass of milk. There was that thing on telly at seven about holidays, and that blonde lady would be on it. Sometimes if it was quiet enough, if Mother was out and there was no cat scratching and meowing at the window, he could imagine she was talking to him, she was his girlfriend, over in some hot place with palm trees and he was going to be going over to join her once he'd finished building their big mansion of a house. They were talking on a special phone with a big video screen. She was describing it to him, the place where they would spend their holidays. You couldn't watch her properly when you were eating your dinner, you had to keep looking down at your plate, and then you'd miss whole seconds of her standing there with her shiny blonde hair, in her clothes that only barely covered what needed covering and, sometimes, clear blue water lapping up around her bum in lucky little waves.

Just as it finished, thank God, Mother arrived in. She wanted to know was it busy below, what kind of form was Packie in, any word of the Scottish lady? Packie's eldest daughter was supposed to have eloped to Scotland with a foreign fella. She was now referred to as the Scottish lady. Like a man who went to work in America for a year or two would forever more be known as the Yank. Packie's daughter used to hang around the co-op some Saturdays, letting on to be helping. All Johnsey ever saw her at was inspecting her fingernails and chewing gum and pressing buttons on her mobile phone. She never really looked at him or talked to him, except once she offered him a Rolo and he said okay (why did you say okay, you spa?) and she held the packet out to him and the blasted Rolo got stuck in the packet and his hand shook like crazy and the Rolo was nearly melted before he got it out and now he could feel his cheeks burning hot again just thinking about it.

Packie had had no time for foreigners before the big elopement, but now he had a special hatred for them. You could nearly feel a heat off of it as it burned inside in him. You'd see them now sometimes, brown-faced people, or even proper blacks, driving through the village, on their way to town to cheat the system, according to Packie, sure tis a great country. If they were outside the co-op at the time, bringing in a delivery or something, Packie would nudge him and point with a tip of his forehead. There'd be a wicked shine from his eyes and it was then you could nearly feel that heat, like Packie's soul was already burning in eternal fire for the sins he was committing in his mind. The foreigners might look back, but you could see nothing in their eyes to give away what they were thinking. They're probably *Hoo-Toos*, Johnsey, Packie would say. He'd spit the words out like you would something you coughed up from your lungs. Probably they killed a rake of *Tootsies* and they're over here now, hiding. Johnsey would laugh and agree away with him, and a picture of the dole boys laughing at Eugene Penrose's stupid jokes would form in his mind and he'd feel sad and ashamed of himself. What in the name of God were a Tootsie and a Hoo-Too, anyway?

They never stopped and came in. Not into the co-op. Sure why would they? Maybe the Spar below did better in the foreigner stakes.

★　★　★

Mother didn't really listen to his answers to her fired-off questions any more. She hardly heard her own questions. She asked them in a listing way that reminded Johnsey of the whole class reeling off the times tables in school years ago. He could have said Sure it was a grand day, Mother, I planted an axe in Packie's forehead, took all the co-op money, went off in the jeep and drove over Eugene Penrose and all the dole boys, killed them all dead, and now that I have the supper ate, I'm off to town to be a cool bigshot and get off with girls. She would probably just stay folding clothes and tightening up and nodding and not seeing him and not hearing him. Good luck so.

He went out in the yard to practise driving. Mother's old Fiesta was going grand, and she let him drive it over and back across the yard. She wouldn't insure him on it, though. Insurance for lads like you now is about twenty thousand pounds, Johnsey. Twenty thousand? Would they know he was thick? Was that one of the questions they asked? Yes, Mister Cunliffe, hmm . . . seeing as you're a bit of a spastic . . . (there would be clicks of computer keys and sighs of impatience) . . . it'll be twenty thousand million billion pounds for basic insurance on that clapped-out heap of old shite. Okay? So stick to your laps of the front yard. All right? You fat gom. *Click.*

He thought better of the driving practice. Mother was complaining the other day about the price of fuel, and anyway it was only a frustration that he couldn't keep going past the gate and roar off down the road. He considered walking up through the long acre and down the river field to the stream. There was something satisfying about the crunching noise your boots made when you walked through grass that was decorated by frost. There was a spot down there by the stream on a rise above the little beach of muck formed by the thirsty cattle, under the weeping willow where you could sit, surrounded by light-green branches, where no one could see you. If you sat still enough you could imagine you were a tree too. No one ever called a tree a spastic or tried to trip it or gave out stink to it for stacking things wrong. Daddy said all life depends on trees. They make the air we breathe.

He was nearly over the stile when he thought of Dermot McDermott, and changed his mind. He was leasing the farm but you'd swear he owned the place, the swagger of him. When Johnsey met him on the land, it was as if he, Johnsey, were a trespasser. He'd ask where was he off to, and he'd never call him Johnsey, only always John. He was too cool for auld *peata* names. And he'd consider Johnsey with a quick up and down of his slitted eyes and a bit of a smirk. He'd be probably thinking Look at this ape, his father dies and he can't manage the bit of a farm that's left behind! I'm here driving my big tractor over his birthright! What a waster!

Mother says people who give their sons names like *Dermot McDermott* are up their own arses. As much as to say we're the *real* McDermotts and our boy is Dermot, son of Dermot, descended directly from the High Kings. Thinking they're two cuts above the *hi-pull-eye* and one cut at least above their neighbours. Mother says the *hi-pull-eye* is the people who live in the council houses outside the village on the end of the Ashdown Road. They nearly all have mongrel dogs and loads of children. Or loads of dogs and mongrel children, Johnsey wasn't sure which Mother said.

★ ★ ★

8

The lock on the door of the slatted house was broken and the wood was warped from dampness and rot, so the door was stuck half open. Even after three years it was strange to have the slatted house empty in January. The cattle made their beds in there every winter; they'd be cosy and warm and safe from the cold rain and the stinging frost, all squashed in together and using each other as big radiators. And their shite would flow away down a pipe all winter and into an underground tank to be sucked back up and spread on the land to feed the grass that they would eat and turn back into milk and shite again. Whenever the teacher would describe the Nativity in school, Johnsey always pictured the stable in Bethlehem as the slatted house that neatly divided the front yard from the big yard, and the three wise men as Daddy, Paddy Rourke and Mister Unthank. The baby Jesus would have been fine and warm and safe in there.

There was enough light allowed in so that Johnsey could see the stout crossbeam that dissected the roof. Would it take his weight? Things was built right in them days, Daddy always said. He was very fat, though. Imagine if he did it arseways and fell on his hole and broke his leg! And Dermot McDermott found him, say. And called Mother. And the fire brigade. And Father Cotter. And then Eugene Penrose and the rest of the dole boys would arrive on after seeing the brigade flying out. The whole village would be standing in the yard for a finish, waiting for a turn to look in the door at the fat eejit on the

9

floor of the slatted house with his leg bursted and cocked at a quare angle, crying like a small child, his face purple and swelled and the rope still tight around his neck, and they'd point and shake their heads and roll their eyes until someone kind would break it up and push them away and try to help him, and their kindness would stab him deeper than the laughter of the rest, because he didn't deserve it, and they'd know it, but be kind anyway.

Father Cotter was that way, and the Unthanks. Packie Collins wasn't. He told Johnsey every day that he was only allowing him work in the co-op out of respect for his father, Lord have mercy on him. He was a *liability*. Johnsey often heard Packie muttering about him to customers, who'd look around and smirk, and if he caught their eye they'd salute him, but in a way that was too friendly, as fake as that cake in the window of the wedding shop inside in town. As fake as a three-pound note, Mother would say. Father Cotter's job was to be nice to people; he worked for God, who gave strict instructions to all to be good and nice. And Mister Unthank was Daddy's great old friend; they'd palled around together since they were small boys. He'd stood at Daddy's coffin for ages in the funeral home, with his hand on the rim, just shaking his head and saying, really softly, *Jack, Jack, Jackie*, and tut-tutting, like Daddy used to over things being wasted and things that weren't right, and Johnsey saw a tear rolling off of Mister Unthank's chin and landing on his

father's cheek, so that it looked like Daddy
himself was crying.

★　★　★

Daddy had always said to be honest. Daddy
wasn't able to tell a lie. Once, years ago, an auld
biddy from the village rang to know would
Mother be able to bake twenty tarts in a hurry
for the ICA show and Daddy told them hold on
and put down the phone and went out to the
chicken coop in the haggard to ask her and
Mother said to tell that old biddy make her own
tarts, no, tell her I'm gone to town and won't be
back till nine but Daddy said No, Sarah. You
know I can't tell a lie. And the way he said it, it
was like the priest saying *and the Word was
made flesh*: it was a fact, a given thing; there
could be no argument. Mother stomped into the
hallway, raging, and had to tell her own lie. Then
she told Daddy that now he had *her* feeling
terrible and she had to go as far as town for a
finish so as to make her lie into truth, and stay
there until nine o'clock to make doubly certain
that truth prevailed that day. That was one of the
things about Daddy: he could make you feel bad
by being so good, so that you *had* to try to be
good like him.

He couldn't think properly abroad in the yard
or around the buildings or even in the dark of
the slatted house. The whole place smelled of
Daddy. Whenever he looked up the yard he
expected to see him striding towards him,
saluting with his stick and full of news even

11

when there was no news. Everything in the yard seemed to have died with him, as though they had only existed to serve him. But still all these things were shaped by his weight and worn by his touch so that no one else could quite fit them: the rut along the yard where he had tramped the same track over and over every day where visitors often stumbled, unaware of its presence until its sides caught their soles; the shiny, paintless edges around the handles of the doors to the slatted house and the milking parlour and the workshop where every day for years on end he had flung them open and closed; the seats of the tractor and the jeep, moulded by the burden of him into a hollow; the very walls of the buildings that seemed to stand now only to honour the memory of his stony strength.

It wasn't good for you, the way this house was now. Even a gom like him could see that. Sadness plus sadness equals more sadness. Sadness begets sadness. The deadness of the yard and the buildings made the air seem thicker and harder to walk through. Dermot McDermott had enough in his own yard and buildings above; he leased the grass only. Anyway, it would have made his heart sick to see that curly-headed fucker flying in and out around Daddy's yard with his big fancy John Deere, destroying the place and taking no care to maintain the integrity of Daddy's world. It would have been an invasion. Better the dead-quiet loneliness that prevailed now than the noisy ignorance of that chap and his fancy machinery. That's the way Daddy would have seen it, Johnsey was certain.

He heard Daddy one time saying he was a grand quiet boy to Mother when he thought Johnsey couldn't hear them talking. Mother must have been giving out about him being a gom and Daddy was defending him. He heard the fondness in Daddy's voice. But you'd have fondness for an auld eejit of a crossbred pup that should have been drowned at birth. He'd be no use for anything only eating and shiteing and he'd be an awful nuisance, but still and all you'd give him the odd rub and a treat, and you'd nearly always be kind to him because it wasn't his fault he was a drooling fool of a yoke. You wouldn't be going around showing him off to people, though, that's for sure.

His bedroom was the best place to think about things. Too much thinking could balls you up rightly. Your mind could start acting like a video player, showing you your own thickness. It was worst when he'd had to talk to people, like one of the auld biddies quizzing him on the way home or in the bakery about Mother or someone stopping him on the street to know how was he and how was his Aunty Theresa and was Small Frank finished his auld exams and he'd stand there and feel his cheeks burning off of him and he'd do his damnedest to try and answer properly and sound like a normal fella but words could make an awful fool of you. What use was talking, anyway? What was ever achieved with words?

Johnsey often thought about girls in his room. He had a dirty magazine that used to belong to Anthony Dwyer, who wasn't quite the gom

Johnsey was, but who had the added hardship of being a meely-mawly with one leg shorter than the other. Looking at Dwyer's magazine often landed him in a sinful place and the thought of doing that made him feel like he sometimes did before walking up to Communion if the Moran girls were sitting near the front in their short skirts: he could feel his heart hammering and jumping and kicking about the place, for all the world as though it was ready to jump up his throat and out his mouth and slap him in the puss before running off on little fat red legs, leaving a bloody trail behind it, shouting Good luck now, fatarse, sure you don't need me, anyway! He had a look out the window and across the yard. No stir abroad. Why would there be?

He imagined Dermot McDermott with a lovely girl in a short skirt and she pinned up against that bollix, trapped, and he saying to her Go on, come on will you and trying to have his rotten way with her and she not wanting to and trying to free herself. Then he imagined he, Johnsey, striding up behind Dermot McDermott and he turning around and Johnsey planting him a box, square on the jaw, and the lovely girl crying Thank you, thank you and Johnsey would put his arms around her and she would suddenly decide she wanted after all to do the dirty things Dermot McDermott had wanted her to do, only with Johnsey, and not the curly fucker who was now prostrated in the muck.

★　★　★

Johnsey had never really spoken to a girl, besides Mother and the aunties and the auld biddies, and they were certainly not real girls like the ones in town or outside Molloy's smoking fags in what Mother called their *bum freezers*. A few hellos and goodbyes and grands and yes pleases and thanks very muches to Packie's daughter and the very odd customer in the co-op who was female; that was it, really.

His parents had talked him into going to a disco once. He didn't know why they were so mad for him to go. It was for the youth only, and being held in a parish hall fifteen miles away. A bus was going from the village, a twenty-five seater, but some would have to stand. The thoughts of that bus, and a hall with girls in it, and Eugene Penrose and all the cool lads laughing and looking at him as if to say where does *he* think he's going, he's not one of us, and the risk of having to talk or being expected to disco dance; Johnsey didn't know why Mother and Daddy were doing this to him. Why couldn't he just stay at home with them, like always, and watch *The Late Late Show* and drink tea and eat buns or currant cake?

Johnsey was thirteen then, his hair was thick and black and wouldn't be told which way to lie, his face was red, his hands were too big, his feet often betrayed him, his voice cracked in his throat and escaped from his mouth all high-pitched or too low and his head shook when he was forced to talk, and surely to God this much misery was too much for one boy to have to bear.

Mother had bought him new trousers especially — they would be for good wear as well, they wouldn't go astray, anyway — and a shirt and a jumper. The jumper was right expensive, and it had a tiny little golfer on it like the ones all the cool lads were wearing. And he had Doc Marten shoes on. Daddy had brought them home for him in a box that said 'Air Wear' on it. But the ones he had brought were too small and he had to carry them back into town and get bigger ones, but he didn't mind, he said it was his own fault — he should have checked.

When he was leaving the house that night for the disco, Mother had brushed his hair back with her hand and kissed him on the forehead and said My little man, off to his first dance. And Daddy drove him down to the village in the jeep, so he felt like a right big man jumping down from the high seat and Daddy winked at him and said Go handy now, leave a few girls for the rest! Johnsey wasn't sure what Daddy meant but it sounded manly and funny and he laughed along and said Good luck, thanks, Dad — he only just remembered not to say *Daddy* while there was a chance any of the cool lads could hear. Daddy had given him a whole fiver on the way down, and it was warm in his hand. The bus was paid for and it was two pounds in, so three pounds of the fiver was all his for spending. What was there to buy at discos? Johnsey could not imagine. Surely there'd be Coca-Cola, anyway. In spite of his nerves, he felt a thrill.

He had been hoping Dwyer would be down at the memorial to wait for the bus so he would

16

have a comrade in spastication. He could still hear Daddy's jeep and smell its fumes when Eugene Penrose sauntered over, flanked by little Mickey Farrell and a lad with fair hair from Fifth Year who was in a fight one day with a fella from the minor team and he drew shocking red blood and won the fight and the fella from the minor team, who was *eighteen*, started crying and the blood solid spurted from his nose.

What are you doing here? Eugene Penrose's hair was long, straight down from his fringe and over his ears. He looked like a right dipstick, Daddy would say. An awful-looking yahoo!

Going to the disco, Johnsey had said.

Are you now? Come on so, come over here and stand with us, old Paddy Screwballs is driving the bus so he'll be ages yet. He's probably above at home picking cling-ons out of his hole.

Johnsey didn't know what to do. Eugene Penrose had talked friendly to him before now and it only ever ended badly. Once, it had lasted a full day, the friendliness, but then he had grabbed his schoolbag going past the church gates and hung it off the high railing and when Johnsey had reached up to get it, Eugene Penrose had pulled down his pants and put a big fist of muck in his underpants and mashed it in with a kick and started roaring that Johnsey had shat in his pants and the whole school-bus crowd saw him with muck all over his arse and on the backs of his legs and he was called Shittyarse Cunliffe for nearly a year after it.

But Johnsey followed Eugene Penrose and

17

little Mickey Farrell with his slanty eyes (Mother had asked Daddy one Sunday coming from Mass, Is that little lad of the Farrells a Mongol, and Daddy had laughed and said No, he's a rat like his father) over to the memorial where all the cool lads were and a few girls acting like they were disgusted with the cool lads but you could tell they weren't, really, and a couple of nervous-looking spastics standing to the side, like bits of auld watery broccoli beside a plate of steak and chips.

Hey, lads, Penrose declared, pulling him by the arm to present him to the rest, Look at Cunliffe's jumper — I'd say his mother knit it and glued a golfer on it!

I'd say his father bought it off the tinkers, someone else volunteered. Johnsey could see his fellow spastics were guffawing away with the cool lads, feeling safely ignored for the minute and trying to gain ground while they could.

Hey, Johnsey Cunt-Lick, don't shit in your pants now, it's only a small bus!

We'll put the fucker in the boot!

Someone grabbed the back of his jumper and yanked the label out and roared *Penneys!*

Johnsey knew his mother hadn't bought his jumper in Penneys; she'd gone to a right expensive place in the city. He knew because he'd heard her telling Daddy it was an awful price and Daddy said Sure what about it and she said It's true, what about it. Then he heard a rip and the two buttons on the shoulder of his jumper landed on the ground. He bent down to pick them up but the jumper-grabber behind still

18

had a grip and there was another rip. Now the neck of his jumper felt too loose and it was slipping down over his shoulder and he wondered how would he explain to Mother and Daddy how his new jumper that was an awful price got destroyed.

Paddy Screwballs arrived and Johnsey's torment, for the moment, was at an end. Surely to God he would be left alone on the bus, with an adult driving it. He sat at the very top, as close to the driver as possible. The other two harmless lads sat across from him. They looked a bit ashamed.

But his sanctuary was soon destroyed: Eugene Penrose landed down beside him, and put a big *mar dhea* friendly arm around his shoulders, and Johnsey had to shove in for him, and little ratty Mickey Farrell and the fair-haired lad landed in the seats behind him and when they started tormenting him again and trying to pull his jumper off of him, old Paddy Screwballs just turned a bit sideways and said Hey, go handy there, and sort of smiled and Johnsey could see he had only three teeth in the front of his stupid old head and he wheezed and coughed and so did the bus and he rammed it in to gear and drove off.

Someone actually lit a fag towards the back of the bus! Even Eugene Penrose was a small bit surprised. But he wouldn't be outdone in the badness stakes. He looked for a fag off of the lad smoking and came back with it lit and started to jab it in Johnsey's face, making him hop the side of his head off the window of the

19

bus every time he flinched. Yerra call a howlt, said Paddy Screwballs, and laughed and coughed. Johnsey could feel the heat of the top of the fag near his skin. He thought of Mother and Daddy asking how he got burned, who did it, and Daddy roaring off in the jeep to Eugene Penrose's house and tackling Eugene Penrose's father over it and there being a big fight and Eugene Penrose calling him *tell-tale-baby-fucker* all day Monday and probably kicking the shite out of him.

Instead of making a hole in Johnsey's face, though, he made a hole in the new jumper. Right in the front, and the place where he touched the fag to the material actually went a bit on fire for a second and that got a great laugh altogether; there were screeches and whoops of delight and when Johnsey jumped up and was beating himself to put out the little flame his fiver escaped from the pocket of his new corduroy trousers and flew away on him and Eugene Penrose grabbed a hold of it and claimed the money as his own. Someone said Ah give it back to hell, but Eugene Penrose said What are you going to do about it? And that was that.

Johnsey imagined Mother in the shop buying him the new jumper, and probably asking the fella working there was it a *cool* jumper now and was it the type all the young lads wore, and his heart broke to think of her thinking so much of him and how happy she'd been over him heading off, all kitted out, like a normal fella.

When they finally arrived at the parish hall where the disco was being held, Johnsey slipped

20

away from the queue. One of the other harmless lads asked where was he going. He didn't answer. He headed for the darkness at the back of the hall where there was a copse of thick-branched trees. He stayed there all night until the disco ended and he heard Paddy Screwballs grinding up the hill. He'd had to retreat further back into the shadows a couple of times because lads came out holding hands with girls and they were kissing each other in among the trees and Johnsey tried to hold his breath and be part of the darkness, because he could imagine if they saw him how the girl would scream and the fella would call him a pervert probably and give him a box.

He heard Bon Jovi singing 'Living on a Prayer', his favourite rock song, and everyone singing along with it, and the DJ was turning off the music at the chorus and it was just the boys and girls at the disco singing and they were nearly louder than the music had been. Then he heard the national anthem and after that they all spilled out and onto the bus. He never had to talk to any girls that night, nor never got to drink a Coca-Cola at the bar like a real man. He threw his burned jumper into the dark among the trees. No one looked at him on the way home, they were all roaring up and down the bus about who felt whose arse and who got a shift and one of the other spastics whispered Where were you all night? and he just told him fuck off.

* * *

21

Dwyer had given him a loan of the dirty magazine when they were pally, years ago. Johnsey had kept it for way longer than Dwyer had meant him to. For a finish, Dwyer had started to get a bit thick over it, but not too thick. A lad in Dwyer's position couldn't afford to be getting too antsy — his heart was in worse shape than his crooked leg by all accounts. He upped and died before Johnsey ever got to give him back his magazine. His heart just stopped beating one night while he was asleep.

His mother and father had been mad about him. Sure why wouldn't they have been mad about their little *crathur*, Mother said to Molly Kinsella the day Dwyer died and a few of the ICA biddies had gathered in Johnsey's mother's kitchen to pick at the tragedy like crows picking at a flungaway snack box. Molly Kinsella allowed that she supposed, throwing her old hairy eyebrows and her witchy chin towards heaven, as much as to say a lad like that couldn't be loved the same as a lad that would be fine and tall and handsome, like Dermot McDermott, and out hurling and having young girls huddled in the bit of a stand mooning over him in little giggling bunches.

Johnsey saw Dermot McDermott kicking his own dog once, above near the Height where the McDermotts' big farm met Daddy's little one. Johnsey had been up foddering but he had left the tractor in the near field and walked a forkful up. He'd heard shouting, a girl's voice calling someone a prick, but by the time Johnsey got a view across to the McDermotts' top field,

Dermot McDermott was alone with their old border collie. A collie was a dog that would love you without fail or compromise. Johnsey saw Dermot McDermott deliver a kick to that lovely old bitch's flank that nearly toppled her and she limped off, crying. He pictured some young lady, after fighting with Dermot McDermott, and she storming off down past their house in a temper, and his people only laughing at her inside in the house as she ran through the yard and he only shaking his head and going on about his business with his big experimental crops that they do be all congratulating him over in the co-op and all questions and telling him he's great. Was that the way with all men and women now?

Not with Mother and Daddy, they only had harsh words the odd time, and then only over silly things like muck getting dragged in through the house and even then Daddy could placate Mother by making her laugh and Johnsey would laugh too at Daddy's clowning and letting on not to know anything about the muck and pretending he was calling the guards because surely an intruder must be at large, and it seemed their world was nearly improved because of the fight. And the Unthanks, Himself and Herself as Mother and Daddy always called them, had a quiet way of moving about each other; you knew they were mad about each other just by the way they laughed at the things the other said and listened when the other was talking and called each other *love* the whole time.

But Johnsey had seen young couples outside

Ciss Brien's and they were certainly not nice to each other. One Friday evening, Johnsey had had to hang back at the pump before the corner because there was roaring and shouting going on just up the road and it made him nervous. A woman was shouting louder than he had ever heard at a fella — Johnsey tried not to listen, but the gist was that they had children and she was going away somewhere and he was meant to be minding the kids and he had promised and here he was drinking every penny he had and that was her money for the *hen*.

A hen? Johnsey couldn't imagine this one buying a hen, with jeans that tight and heels that high. As he chanced walking past he saw her face clearly; it had black rivers running down it and your man was a fine fat lad like himself, but with a tattoo of a cross on his neck. Out from the city, like a lot were, rehoused by the County Council. The cross-tattoo lad was smoking his fag away and ignoring the woman in the tight jeans and for a finish she just stood there going You bastard, and when Johnsey walked past trying to be invisible she said What are you looking at, you spastic, in that singsong townie voice.

Johnsey felt aggrieved that she should know this about him. The cross-tattoo lad seemed glad she had a distraction from him. He's only a retard, he declared. Johnsey picked up his pace. A *retard*. Ree-tard. Lovely, coming from a big fat lad with a cross drawn on his neck that wouldn't mind his own children, besides drinking all the money for the hen. Johnsey wouldn't do that if he had a wife, even a wild-looking one with jeans stuck to her arse; he'd mind her and his children and bring all his wages home and do silly things to make them all laugh. Thinking of those jeans and the bit of pink frill he could see peeping over the top of them made Johnsey think of the magazine again. And what if one of those who had passed away was watching him and he inside in the jacks, interfering with himself? The dead are all around us, according to Father Cotter. They're having a right old laugh at me, so.

Johnsey went down to the front room where Mother was watching the news and knitting something with no shape yet, and the big brown clock ticked and tocked the night slowly away. They'd hardly ever used the good room before Daddy died. If they were all watching telly, they'd sit on the long, battered green couch that was hidden away near the back kitchen, out of sight of visitors when not in use. Daddy would drag it into service and position it in front of the hearth, directed in by Mother like he was reversing a trailer in the yard, and Johnsey would sit in the middle between them and they'd look at a film or a comedy and Mother would make tea during one of the ad breaks and bring over tart and cream on a tray and you couldn't get better than that. But now it was all the good room with Mother. That long, battered couch was covered in boxes and bits and bobs that had no business on a couch. It wouldn't have been balanced right, anyway, without Daddy. There'd have been too much empty space on it, and that empty space would draw out your sadness like the vacuum cleaner draws out dust from behind the television: you'd have forgotten it was there until you went rooting around for it.

When bedtime came he was glad to say goodnight to Mother and retreat upstairs to think. A man couldn't think about things with his mother in the room — it was hard enough thinking of things to say to a woman who had hardly any words left for the world, only lonesome thoughts and muttered prayers.

The cross one in the tight jeans had looked a bit like the girls in Dwyer's dirty magazine. Johnsey couldn't believe they were fully real, them wans. How could a part of a woman look so strange, like an alien's face, and yet make you not be able to stop looking at it?

★   ★   ★

Johnsey liked thinking about the stories Daddy used tell him before he went to sleep. A rake of his great-uncles were priests in Scotland and America and Canada. They joined the priesthood and exiled themselves as penance for taking the lives of so many Black and Tans years ago during the War of Independence. Daddy's father was only very young, the youngest of six boys and a girl, and he and his sister would be warming blocks all night and placing them in the lads' empty beds, down low where their feet would be if they were not patrolling the countryside shooting Englishmen, so when they came home and tore their clothes off and jumped into their beds, their feet would warm quick enough so that if they were raided, their

26

mother would shout Sure look, sir, feel those boys' feet, they've been in their beds since sunset, for they've all to be up at cockcrow. And sure enough the rotten bastard would beat them from their beds with the butt of his dirty English gun and line them up for his inspection and they would act like they'd just been dragged from the deepest of sleep and their toes toasty, and that trick saved many a young rebel's life.

The English officer would leave them their lives but before they went away he'd let the Black and Tan bastards loose about the place and they'd try to flush the Blessed Virgin down the toilet and they'd take the holy picture out to the yard and fling it on the ground and piss all over Our Lord and God only knows what other depravities were visited upon holy things before finally the great-uncles won their war and John Bull and his savage legion fecked off home out of it. Johnsey thought of their bravery and boldness and wondered why had he not the same daring. Hadn't he the same blood? Those great-uncles he never met would have no trouble talking up for theirselves or getting girls to do the things described in Dwyer's American magazine. They'd beat the head off of the likes of Eugene Penrose for sport.

And what about Granddad? Sure didn't he grow up just as brave, but by then the Free State had been established and the Irish had turned their guns on each other and then made up again, kind of, and his brothers had scattered to the four winds. He drove his motorbike across Lough Derg once, when the lake was iced over

27

completely, from Youghal Quay the whole way across to County Clare, just to see could it be done without a fella falling through, and he made it clear across, where he drank a brandy and smoked a fag and doubtless talked to a load of Clare girls and turned around and flew it the whole way back and was hailed a hero. Maybe you had to have brothers to be brave; they would knock toughness into you. Granddad married a woman so beautiful that people — men *and* women — stood and stared at her with their mouths open, wondering could such a creature really be real. And Daddy was another hero, loved and feared in near equal measure by all who knew him. And what about Daddy's brother, Uncle Michael, who was long dead and nearly never talked about? He fell off of scaffolding beyond in London and was killed and he only twenty-one. He was *beautiful*, Mother said once. That was a funny thing to say about a man. He could have charmed the birds right out of the trees, by all accounts.

All about him in that house were the ghosts of heroes, and here lay he, a lonesome gom, letting them all down.

February

January was lonely and slow and drawn out as a rule, no matter what Mother said about it. The first day of February is the first day of spring, Daddy used to say, as if you could dictate to a season when it was to start. More would contend spring began in March, but the way Daddy used to say it, looking up at the sky as if to see was God listening, to remind him to send the new season, his words would nearly make the world warm up.

The calving would always start in earnest at the start of February. One year, when he was only a small boy, five or six, Daddy and Johnsey and Mother gave half a night outside in the barn with a cow whose calf was coming and the calf was breech. That meant she was turned the wrong way. She was trying to reverse into the world, Daddy said. Daddy reached right in to the poor roaring heifer's insides and pulled her calf out by the legs and set it gently on the hay. She shook and wobbled and tried to walk, and then she lay down and died. She was too early, Daddy said. Johnsey cried for the little early calf but Mother told him that calf was steeped lucky. A certain number of calves had to be brought up to heaven each spring because God had a beautiful farm above around the stars where they could live and play and never know cold nor hardship and that had made him feel better.

The air was cold but soon the sun would get over the effort of climbing up from behind the mountains and would start its short day's work before slipping back down below the earth again. Johnsey liked the way the world looked and felt on a cold, clear early morning: crisp and clean and seemingly emptied of all other life. On his walk to the village Johnsey often imagined that he was the last man left alive after some mad professor let off a bomb that made every other human dissolve into dust and there was only himself left and a handful of young girls like the ones on *Home and Away*. Johnsey would have to save them from the animals that had turned wild from hunger. He'd march about the place with Daddy's shotgun strapped to his back and the cartridge belt around his waist, and the young ladies would follow behind him and adore him, their saviour.

Daddy's shotgun was still kept just inside the attic trapdoor at home, asleep in its leather holder, on a soft bed of insulation. You could smell a mixture of wood and metal and oil off of it when you picked it up. A Winchester, under-and-over, two black sideways eyes. A cold and heavy thing, you could nearly feel its dark weight through the ceiling. He often thought of the shotgun these days. Daddy had showed him how to fire it properly when he was fourteen, gripped firm, snug against his shoulder. Then he had taken him to the river field and pointed out a rabbit, cocked up on top of a rise, sniffing the air. He had helped him with his aim and told him be steady, to aim for the head, to take his time. When they collected the dead rabbit and Daddy congratulated him on his fine clean shot, he'd have given the whole world and everything in it to go back three minutes in time and leave that little rabbit to his lovely happy spring day in the meadow.

Mother knew well, when they arrived back to the house. She felt the pain in his heart, just as if it was her own; Look at him, Jack, for God's sake, he's as white as a ghost. He's not cut out for that type of thing.

Sometimes you didn't know how you would feel about doing a thing until you went and did it. And then it's too late; you can never ever undo it.

★ ★ ★

The Johnston brothers who delivered fruit and vegetables to the co-op were there before him, one of them hopping from one foot to the other and clapping his hands together like it was feckin Antarctica or something and the other sitting in the cab of their big green lorry smoking a fag. The hoppy one had a nose that no man's face should have to support. His back was bent, as if the burden of that massive snout was forcing his head forward and down towards the ground. Johnsey often caught himself staring at it. Then he'd realize his mouth was open and the big-nosed brother had stopped talking and a blind man could see Johnsey had been staring at

31

his nose, but there was a word for the effect that that nose had, Johnsey knew . . . *hypnotic!* That was it. Imagine being *hypnotized* by a nose!

If Daddy had ever seen that fellow's big auld Dublin nose, Johnsey knew, he would have made a great skit out of it. He would have said something to Johnsey like I bet that lad *nose* a lot about vegetables! And he would have dug Johnsey with his elbow and said it again, and then Johnsey would have gotten it and he would feel weak from laughing. And then at home Daddy would have to describe the nose to Mother and the way he would describe it would be so funny, Johnsey would get to have the whole big laugh again.

The other lad was lanky and sneaky-looking with a head of tight curls and long fingers gone yellow from the fags. He would always try to make a fool of Johnsey and would say things like he needed a loan of a skirting ladder or a glass hammer or a sky hook and would Johnsey ask Packie for him, but Johnsey was wise to all of them by now, he'd heard it all before. While he was talking and trying to cod him he'd be looking over at Bignose and winking and Johnsey would try to laugh with them but really it wasn't that funny.

When Packie arrived in he was like a dog, ranting and raving about the government and he straight away started pulling and dragging at the four-stone bags that Johnsey had stacked up lovely and neat. Those sneaky bollixes are trying to pull strokes, did you weigh them bags, no you didn't, sure what do you care, you get the same pay no matter what, take out them weighing scales, throw those bags up one by one, Lord it's a sin to have to pay you good money to stand there like a gorilla scratching yourself.

Packie was forever going on about the wages he was forced to pay Johnsey and the terrible injustice that was being perpetrated on the small business with this *minimum wage* malarkey. Well if it came in he could sing for it, Packie said. There was a thing in there in that law that said lads without their full faculties weren't entitled to it, anyway.

Johnsey wasn't exactly sure what *faculties* were but he knew there were no bits missing off of him on the outside, so it must be something inside him that Packie thinks is not right and stops him from getting the minimum wage. Johnsey knew what minimum meant: a point, below which you could not go. There weren't as many flies on Johnsey as Packie made out. He knew all about the new law coming in. But what about it, Packie knew no law only his own, and points below which you may not go would not apply to Johnsey.

★ ★ ★

The day dragged on and on like Tuesdays often do — it's a nowhere day, Daddy used to say — it's not at the start of the week or in the middle or the end, it's just the long day before the hump. The hump is Wednesday. Wednesday always made Johnsey think of a little bridge that you had to run over to get from one end of the

33

week to the next. Johnsey's weekdays were nearly all the same: up in the morning, in to work, lunch in the bakery, back to work, finish work, get dog's abuse on the way home from work, try not to cry, home, eat the dinner, look at television with silent Mother, up to bed, read his book, fall asleep thinking about Daddy, or girls, or hearing back his own thick words, and off we go again, dead tired and full of emptiness.

At lunch he would go to the Unthanks' bakery and Himself would give him a lovely roll still warm from his oven and he'd put ham and cheese in it, and give him a Danish pastry for after, or a jam doughnut. The thought of the bakery made the day slow down even more; the warm bread smell and the little tables set out with the red and white tablecloths, the look of the Unthanks, and they smiling at him from behind the long wood counter, the pictures on the wall that hadn't changed since Johnsey's childhood and the feeling of gentleness that was always there. Even when the place was full and people were sitting drinking their tea and eating their sandwiches or cakes or buns in every seat and all along the window on the high stools and there was a big queue at the counter as well for the fresh warm bread, there was always somewhere to sit for Johnsey, because Herself would bring him in to her own kitchen and always make a big song and dance of him. It was never like the chipper, where sometimes fellas jumped in front of Johnsey and once, after Johnsey had paid for his burger and chips and was walking out the door and his mouth was watering just thinking about the treat ahead of him, a lad kicked his bag from his hands and it flew through the air and landed in the middle of the street and his chips were everywhere, all over the ground, and a dog ran straight over and ate his burger in one big gulp.

★   ★   ★

There was an old girl who worked in the bakery who was a bit daft — Mother called her Mary with the Cod Eye — she never looked in your face when she was talking and her voice was squeaky and small and reminded Johnsey of a cartoon mouse. Now *she* didn't have all her faculties, Johnsey was certain. He didn't think the Unthanks would roar at her about the minimum wage, though, and how she could sing for it.

Johnsey was sitting at the Unthanks' kitchen table and Mary with the Cod Eye brought him in his roll and his tea. There was a beaded curtain between the kitchen and the counter area and an opening in the long counter directly across from the curtain. Johnsey could see out to where the tables were. People couldn't really see back in, because it was darker in the Unthanks' kitchen than it was outside in the shop.

Old Paddy Rourke was sitting at a small table on his own. Every time he lifted his teacup to his lips, it shook and clacked against the saucer as he put it back down. It looked like a toy teacup and saucer from a doll's house in Paddy Rourke's big hand. Johnsey wondered why he didn't ask Mary with the Cod Eye for a mug altogether, like some of the louder men did. She should have had the cop on not to make him ask, anyway.

Paddy Rourke was attacked once, at home in his own yard. A van pulled up and three fellas got out and ran in around his yard and house and started to load machinery into their van, a cement mixer and a chainsaw and a few other bits. They must have known Paddy had no phone, Daddy said. When Paddy came out and let a roar out of him, one of them hit him in the face with a shovel and they must have all had a go at kicking him. He was inside in the hospital for nearly two months. Daddy said Paddy's big mistake was coming out to them without his gun. He should have gave them both barrels, Daddy said. He should have come out shooting and let the law be damned. Towards the end of the summer where he faded away and died, Daddy said to Johnsey to always look out before going out to a visitor and never to go out to the yard to a tinker without his shotgun, loaded and locked. Johnsey didn't know would he be able to point a gun at a man, though. What if it went off and blew your man's head off by mistake? And then it turned out he was only selling frozen meat or something?

Paddy looked smaller ever since he had gotten that beating off the tinkers. He always looked kind of embarrassed now too, as if he thought it was a failing, a shameful thing, almost, to have been beaten like that. Until the cancer and the tinkers came, Daddy and Paddy Rourke were big, tough men. They wouldn't have allowed themselves to be tormented daily by the likes of Eugene Penrose. It took three big buck tinkers to fell Paddy Rourke, and he was now standing again, and three kinds of cancer to do for Daddy: he got it in his stomach, lungs and brain. *Three kinds* imagine!

And he nearly bested them too.

★ ★ ★

Eugene Penrose's campaign started in primary school, and then went on through secondary school, even though Johnsey went to the Tech for the last two years and Eugene Penrose to the Christian Brothers, as the Tech gave Eugene Penrose the road for constantly acting the little prick. They still had to get the same bus home from town. Then when they were all finished with school Johnsey's trials were temporarily ended by Eugene Penrose's disappearance. He went to England to work for his uncle as a plasterer. There was talk of him having to go on account of trouble inside in town one night where a girl got interfered with. But he arrived home after a few years (not even his own uncle could stand the rotten little bastard, Mother said) and Johnsey's heart broke to see him bowling down the middle of the village with his big red head and his vicious smile.

He got a job in the meat factory over in Kill, but that place ground to a halt two years ago and ever since he seemed to spend his days hanging around the IRA memorial in the village with a small crew of gougers, spitting and shouting and making Johnsey run a daily gauntlet as he passed. Eugene Penrose seemed to hate Johnsey even more now that he had a job and Eugene Penrose hadn't. Johnsey wondered how big a sin it was to want someone to be dead, and worse, to actually want to be the one to kill them? He imagined himself getting an arm around Eugene Penrose's throat and squeezing him in a headlock until his mouth was shut forever.

The worst thing was, they had all been great old pals as small boys, starting off. In Junior Infants and Senior Infants and First and Second Class it had been Johnsey, Dwyer, Eugene Penrose, Seanie Mac, Murty Donnell, Billy Hassett, Cookie Ryan, Joe Counihan, Conor Quinn and a few more. Then divisions started when blow-ins arrived from town and the boys started to listen to what was being said at home and to look at each other differently. So the sons of bigshots started to pal around just with each other, and the sons of labourers and the blow-ins from town formed their own, separate groups. Dwyer was the most gammy and so occupied a group of his own. Johnsey felt sorry for Dwyer but not sorry enough to be his champion. He had enough troubles of his own being the biggest and clumsiest and mumbliest.

★ ★ ★

Most lads their age had women now. Johnsey would see them around the place, driving cars with girls in them, walking through the village holding hands, all going to the pub together after matches in big happy groups — some lads were even *married*. One fella who had been a year *behind* Johnsey in school had a big huge house built abroad in Roskeeda, but his father was a bigshot who bought and sold huge tracts of land like another man would buy and sell cattle or sheep.

They were all the one with the *piseogs*, that crowd, Mother said. Sure, they came from nothing. It's no bother to have it all on this earth when you give yourself over to the devil. Johnsey wondered did Mother really believe that, or was it just the way she had a bee in her bonnet always about the *bigshots*. But Johnsey had heard stories of distant relations who had broken eggs left in haycocks and their store of hay would rot, and turned milk thrown around milking parlours and cows would only issue sourness, and stillborn lambs left against back doors and whole herds would fall to disease and have to be destroyed. One old relation beyond in Holyford had to go to the Land Commission years ago it got so bad, to be given an idle farm miles from his home. He had to leave his birthright to the neighbours who were in league with the devil and had forced him out with their dark tricks.

As bad as it would be to have dealings with the devil, how much could it jeopardize his immortal soul to just *know* if there was a way of making Eugene Penrose leave him alone for once? He had even been at Daddy's funeral. He shook Johnsey's hand at the removal and his hand was limp and sweaty. He just smirked at Johnsey and said nothing. His father followed behind, red-faced with small, darting eyes. Daddy used to give that man work, years ago. But Daddy would never have a man feeling beholden. Fair was fair. The likes of the Patsy Penroses of this world, though, you could give them your last penny and they'd come back for your purse. And while they were drinking the wages you gave them, they'd be cursing you to your neighbours.

★ ★ ★

Daddy had been *riddled* by all accounts. Johnsey had heard one of the ICA biddies saying it in the front room. When he went in with the stomach pains last winter, they opened him up, took one look and closed him again. Sent him straight home. Nothing they could do. He was riddled, the auld crathur. He. Was. RIDDLED.

You could be riddled with bullets if you were in a Western. An old chair could be riddled with woodworm. And you could be riddled with cancer. If you were riddled, you could put your head between your legs and kiss your arse goodbye. Johnsey imagined Daddy's insides, black and full of holes. He had smelt Daddy's breath towards the end — it was like rot. Daddy was like a chestnut someone had opened. A conker that was peeled, it looked fine and hard for a while but then got hollow and dried out and shrivelled up and dead-looking.

If Johnsey started to think about that in the co-op, say, or in the bakery, when there were people around, he would feel a pain in the bottom of his throat and he would not be able to swallow his own spit. He would as a rule be able to stop the tears from falling, by blinking like a madman and breathing in deeply and holding his breath, but that discipline had taken a good few weeks to master after Daddy died. If he was on his own, walking the quiet road home or above in his room, he would often not notice his tears until he felt them puddling at his chin. He wished he could be hard and closed in like some men seemed to be. He remembered Raphael Clancy when his young lad got caught in a drive shaft and killed — he stood above in the church like a thing made of rock, he was ghostly white and had no words for anyone, but no womanly tears or sobbing either. You wouldn't see big hard men like him stumbling along the road weeping, or standing at his father's deathbed keening like a banshee.

This couldn't be kept up, though, this way he had of seeing only blackness lately. How could a man's life just be made up of sadness over his dead father and worry over his shrinking mother and fear over his childhood enemy jumping out at him from behind the stupid IRA memorial every evening? Mother *was* shrinking too. She had gone from fully upright two years ago to a small bit stooped over just after Daddy died to a little hunched-over thing, like a question mark, wrapped in sorrow and silence. She used to be all movement and talk and baking and crossness, you often could hardly see her for the cloud of flour around her or the speed she was moving at, nor hardly hear for her giving out and laughing and stories about this one saying this and that

41

one wearing that and the other one after being seen *again* inside in town with that fella from the Silvermines who left his wife. It wasn't until Daddy was buried, when the house was at last empty of people who came full of condolences and left full of sandwiches, apple tart, tea and drink that Mother at last came to a dead stop. Now she only moved slowly and with no great purpose, her eyes were cast down at the ground as a rule, and she rarely went farther than the graveyard above on the Height where Daddy lay.

Sympathy doesn't last forever. Like a pebble thrown in a river, it's a splash and a ripple and gone. He had often overheard Mother and the biddies discussing wans whose husbands had died. Yerra, she'd want to be getting over it now, they'd say, it's been a year and she still going around with a long face like the weight of the feckin world is on her. Once there was a Christmas between the death and the present you had no right to be olla-goaning any more. Sympathy, it seemed, began to run out of steam after a few months and expired completely within a year. She has the Christmas over her now she'll be grand, they'd say, as if it was a hard and fast rule, like not eating for the hour before Communion. Imagine what they were saying about her! Signs on the confabs that used to be held regularly in Mother's kitchen no longer took place. They were clucking and tutting in some other kitchen now, and Mother was the auld quare wan who'd want to be getting over it.

Eugene Penrose and his little band were nowhere to be seen on the way home. Johnsey's heart lightened. There was a nip, but it was still lovely and sunny. The sun had something in it that cheered you up. That was a true thing, not something makey-up. Daddy used to read science magazines sometimes. Mother often said he could have been *anything* he had such a brain. But only bigshots could afford to send their children off to the university in those days. Anyway, his parents had needed him at home. How, Johnsey wondered, did a man like that manage to have such a dud of a son? Miss Malone had taught them all about *sexual reproduction* in secondary school. Men shot billions of sperms into women. One sperm swam up the whole way to the egg. How in the name of God had Johnsey managed to win that swimming race? All those other sperms must have been quare gammy. How many billions of sperms had Johnsey shot into tissues and flushed down the jacks? Were they all tiny little half-humans? Surely you could end up in hell for such unbridled slaughter.

When Johnsey turned in the gate, a lone magpie stood in the middle of the yard, eyeballing him. Johnsey searched in vain for a second that would bring him joy, then waved away the lone magpie's cargo of bad luck. The magpie shook his head and hopped away. He didn't even *fly* away. Even the birds of the sky knew he was harmless.

43

Mother was not in the kitchen. And she had no dinner left for Johnsey. One time it was all he could do to finish the dinners Mother gave him: cuts of beef or lamb drowned in gravy the way he loved it, creamy mash, turnip and carrot bound together with butter and salt, fresh tart or crumble with custard for afters. Or salty bacon and curly cabbage with creamy dollops of white sauce — his favourite and Daddy's too. Johnsey had never known a day without any dinner cooked until now. The quality had been in decline since Daddy died, fair enough, but a complete lack of any dinner was never before countenanced. A fist of worry clenched Johnsey's gut. The house felt cold, wrong.

★ ★ ★

He found Mother lying in the front room. She had on her green dress that she often wore to Mass. One of her legs was straight and one was bent at the knee, as if for modesty's sake. Her arms were out from her sides like Christ on the Cross. Her head was turned to the side. She was looking at something under the couch, it seemed, and she was surprised by whatever it was, because her mouth was open like an O and her lips had turned blue from the excitement. If Mother had wanted to lie down, why had she not lain on the couch or gone upstairs to bed? Mother. Get up. *Mother.* His mouth was opening but no sound was coming out. Like in a dream where dark shapes are coming at you and

your legs won't move and you try to scream but
you can't.

★　　★　　★

Later that night, Father Cotter told him he had
been very calm throughout his ordeal. He had
been sitting on the floor looking down at his
mother when the ambulance came. He'd had
one of her hands in his. He had closed her eyes.
He had answered all of their questions. She had
been dead for at least five hours, the doctor said.

March

Christ, there's a great stretch in the evenings. March already, imagine! March comes in like a lion and goes out like a lamb. Bejaysus, the year is pure-solid flying. The worst of the cold is gone, anyway, thanks be to God.

Daddy would make these same observations every year at the start of March. He would also give his predictions for the weather to come. The quantity and location of slugs and beetles and other creepy-crawlies; the hop of a cock robin; the zigzag of rabbits and foxes across fields; the colour of the evening shadow cast by the Arra Mountains on the fields that cuddled up to their feet; the early or late departure or return of migrating birds and the height of their flight: all of these things and more spoke to Daddy of the temperament of the coming season in a secret language of signs and signals.

Yerra stop spoutin', Mother would tell him, and roll her eyes towards heaven. But then you would hear her repeating Daddy's predictions *word for word* to her friends the ICA biddies while they drank tea and ate currant cake and clucked in the kitchen and they'd Ooh and Ah in wonder at Daddy's knowledge and skill and nod to each other knowingly and say Now! How's it them feckers in the Met Office and all their smartness couldn't tell us that?

Loneliness covers the earth like a blanket. It flows in the stream down through the Callows to the lake. It's in the muck in the yard and the briars in the haggard and the empty outbuildings are bursting with it. It runs down the walls inside of the house like tears and grows on the walls outside like a poisonous choking weed. It's in the sky and the stones and the clouds and the grass. The air is thick with it: you breathe it into your lungs and you feel it might suffocate you. It runs into hollow places like rainwater. It settles on the grass and on trees and takes their shapes and all the earth is wet with it. It has a smell, like the inside of a saucepan: scraped metal, cold and sharp. When it hits you, it feels like a rap of a hurl across your knuckles on a frosty winter's morning in PE: sharp, shocking pain, but inside you, so it can't be seen and no one says sorry for causing it nor asks are you okay, and no kind teacher wants to look at it and tut-tut and tell you you'll be grand, good lad.

But you know if another man stood where you're standing and looked at the same things he wouldn't see it or feel it. He'd see that the fields are only wet with dew and the walls only running because the vents are blocked with dirt and grime and it's Virginia creeper climbing the house that people used to stop to admire for its lovely, fiery colours on their passage up the yard towards the front door. So it only exists in your head. It only occupies a tiny space. Is it even an inch squared? Probably not. How big is a feeling?

47

Not even as big as one of them atoms that the science teacher used to be on about. It's nothing and everything at the same time.

The world doesn't change, nor any thing in it, when someone dies. The mountains keep their still strength, the sun its heat, the rain its wetness. Blackbirds still hop and flutter about the back lawn, fighting over worms. The cat still screeches and paws at the back window for her grub. Bees still dance about the flowers and the apple trees, always searching, searching. There's an awful cruelty in the business of nature, in the brutal sameness of things. The sky was the same blue the day after Daddy died as it was the day before; the uncaring rain didn't stop while they buried Mother, only bucketed ignorantly down and ran in muddy rivers from the Height to the road below.

★ ★ ★

Eugene Penrose and the dole boys relented for a while. If they were at the pump or the memorial of an evening, they left him walk past unhindered. But he knew they'd soon tire of their nod to common decency and resume slagging and ciffling and tormenting him. Even Packie was tolerably nice to him for a few weeks. The Unthanks gave him a fine lunch every day in the bakery, and a few times Herself bent down and kissed him on top of his head while he was eating. Whenever she did, he felt like crying again. She gave him his dinner every day as well in her own kitchen for the first while, then after a week or so, when he was back working in the co-op, she gave him a plate of something every evening, wrapped in tinfoil to carry home and heat up in the microwave.

Mother had nearly never used the microwave. It was a present from one of the aunties. Mother said the old witch was too scared to use it and so dumped it on her. She said it could give you any kind of disease, how would you know? She said some lady had stood in front of one while it was working and it fried her liver and she died in screaming agony. The first time Johnsey turned it on by himself, carefully following the instructions Himself had written on an envelope for him, he stood well clear. When it pinged to tell him it was finished, he nearly jumped out of his skin. Himself said if a microwave *had* fried someone's liver, it was years and years ago, when they were invented first and no seals were put on them. Now, the microwaves could not escape. Johnsey wasn't fully convinced. He always opened and shut the door fierce fast. He didn't want runaway microwaves flying about the place and frying bits of him.

The Unthanks had suggested he come down and stay with them. He couldn't. It would be just too embarrassing. Among other mortifications, he would have to use their toilet. Imagine the two lovely gentle people trying to pretend they didn't notice the terrible stink from the great ape they had invited into their home! It wouldn't be fair on them. Probably, if he stayed there any length, he wouldn't use the toilet at all. Like the time Daddy's cousin from New Jersey in

America and his scary blonde wife and their wild children had come to stay in the house when Johnsey was twelve. They were *touring Europe*, thank you very much (the cut of them, Mother said, that fella hadn't a seat in his pants growing up and he going around now *touring Europe* for himself! I ask you. How's it he wasn't staying inside in town in the new hotel so, besides issuing himself an invitation to land his whole family on top of them if he was so swanky?), and they stayed a week and a bit and he never shat the whole time and was doubled up in agony for a finish. When they were safely gone and he finally went, his hole nearly burst open with the concrete block he had to force out through it.

Or, he could run up home. He still couldn't imagine, though, being a guest in someone's house, even the Unthanks who he had known and loved dearly since childhood. He would be a big, smelly, sweaty nuisance and they would hate the sight of him and want him to leave. Johnsey didn't even know how they made themselves be so nice to him during his daily lunch.

★　★　★

Johnsey had gotten used to being sad after Daddy died. This extra sadness was just like taking more weight forking hay: you built it up gradually so that when your burden increased, your muscles were ready and you would not collapse under it. Mother had spent two and a bit years wrapped in a cloak of sadness, hardly talking and, he saw now, only waiting around

50

until her time came to join Daddy. How could she have just upped and left him like that? Granted, he was no great prize of a chap; he had never given her any reason to be below in the Post Office boasting about him like some women who would talk out loud in the queue for fear anyone would not accidentally overhear about their sons who were doing Masterses, or just finishing their accountancy exams, or were abroad in Australia for a year, sure didn't he deserve a bit of fun after studying so hard for years, blah de blah de blah.

But he was surprised at Mother all the same. She had sure left him in the lurch. It felt like she had planned this behind his back, to go and meet Daddy and leave him on his own. Like all those muttered prayers were her talking to him under her breath all along, arranging her departure. Was he not even worth staying on this earth for? He felt a bit annoyed with Daddy too, truth be told. It was like he was in on it, somehow. Were the two of them watching over him at least, like Father Cotter told him? Sometimes he wished he could see their ghosts, but then he'd probably run away screaming if it actually happened. Or roar shouting at them for leaving him behind.

That was something else about being totally alone that Johnsey knew he would not be able to stand for very long more: the feeling that he was *not* alone. The house creaked and moaned at night, as it always did, but before he used to always hear Mother's breathing and sighs from down the hallway as well. The only feeling of real

51

comfort he had in the two and a bit years of Mother living and Daddy dead were on nights when he was in bed before her and she was foostering about downstairs and praying (or talking to Daddy?) under her breath: the old house would carry her sounds down to his ear and he could drift away knowing she was at least there in body, and she might come round eventually and laugh again, or gossip, or give out at least. Now, every mouse-squeak became boot leather chafing against itself as someone crept along the hall towards his room; every clink or clunk or faint tinkle became an enemy arming himself, or a demon preparing to suck his life out through his mouth and carry away his soul to hell. These thoughts often became thoughts about the crossbeam in the slatted house and the rope on the hook in the back kitchen. How big of a sin could it really be to want to be with your mother and father in heaven? Why would God want him to persevere with this empty misery? Father Cotter says He has a plan for us all. Thanks, God, for the great plan.

★ ★ ★

Up in the morning, cereal and toast, down to the village to work, lunch in the bakery, home past Eugene Penrose and his monkeys who were starting to settle back nicely into their old ways now, heat up dinner, television, into bed. Long nights trying to push black thoughts from his mind so he may sleep. Weekends were worse. He used to love them. He and Daddy would be out doing jobs all day Saturday; they'd go to a match most Sundays in summer and maybe go to the cinema in winter, or watch a film at home, or a soccer match on the television. The fire would always be roaring. Mother would always do a great spread on Sundays and she'd have baked on Saturday so there would be an array of desserts. Now Saturday was a day of sleeping until the middle of the day, waking up from savage dreams to a cold, dead house, trying to sort out laundry, going to the village for a burger and chips and hoping there'd be a dirty film on Channel 4 that night. Sunday was a day of going to early Mass and sitting there thinking blasphemous thoughts about God and his quare plans, eating his dinner with the Unthanks and feeling guiltier each time over abusing their hospitality by imposing his big, lummoxing self on their cosy Sabbath. And any evening, with no warning, Aunty Theresa might drag in with mousy Nonie and Theresa's cross, bored husband Frank to tell him he'd have to start making plans and sort the house out and would they go up now and go through Sarah's things and he would have to stutter and mumble his way into putting them off because if you let crows pick at your dead dog's eyes you could no longer tell yourself he was only asleep.

When Mother died, the Unthanks and his aunties and a small army of biddies had done everything. They had sorted out the business with the coroner and roared down the phone at people to know what was the delay in releasing the body and explained gently to him how things take longer when a person dies at home with no doctor present. They had cleaned the house from top to bottom and baked and made sandwiches and bought liquor and instructed the undertakers and sorted out Johnsey's suit and tie and even polished his shoes for him. They had somehow managed to work out how everything would be paid for; there was a folder of pages and bank books and what have you in a box in the small room upstairs where Daddy used to curse over his accounts with his glasses sliding down his nose and they had tightened up that mess of documents and explained things to Johnsey and their explanations entered one ear and spilled out of the other, their passage unimpeded by any form of understanding.

He'd had to sign a few bits and pieces relating to God only knows what and he did so in his best handwriting, all joined up and slanted forward. They had said sure nobody could organize all these things on their own, a person needed time to come to terms with the shock, it was an awful burden of grief, losing both parents like that in such a short space of time. What they really meant was: Look, you're a bit of a gom, so go on now and leave us to get on with the important business of burying your mother properly and sorting out her affairs for you. Okay? Good lad. Go off upstairs now and say a few prayers or pull yourself or do whatever the hell it is imbeciles do in the confines of their own bedrooms.

It wasn't a *terrible* thing that people who were being kind sometimes couldn't do it without making you feel like it was because you were a bit of a God-help-us. They wouldn't mean it, but it would be obvious from their manner; the way they'd smile sadly and nod at you and then look away and smile sadly at someone else as much as to say Ah sure, the poor *crathur*, he hasn't a clue or a hand to wipe his arse nor a dust of sense. Not the Unthanks, though. Definitely not. They made you feel like *you* were doing *them* a favour by letting them help you. Or Father Cotter, but then that was part of his covenant with God, to be kind to all without prejudice. Most people wanted something in return for their kind help, if only the sense of having given of themselves selflessly, that might make their bed feel softer or their sleep come easier, or the gates of heaven swing open faster when their time came. Johnsey could see it in the secret glances of the ICA biddies and the aunties and the few bigshot women who flocked and squawked and pecked about him at the time of his parents' deaths. He'd have preferred them to stay away than to enter his house and act like they were abroad in Africa saving little black babies from starvation.

★ ★ ★

Now that mother wasn't here to be hurt by him, wasn't it just common sense that he should carry out his plans for the rope and the crossbeam in the slatted house? What in the name of God was the purpose of a great clumsy yoke who had relinquished his father's land to the sneaky neighbours without argument and couldn't really hold a conversation without feeling like he was going to burst into flames and who had nothing of any interest to say, anyway, because he had never been anywhere without his parents to mind him, who had never kissed a girl nor stood his ground to bullies nor drove a car past the gate?

He had gone as far as taking Daddy's old rope from the back kitchen. He had thrown it over the crossbeam and climbed to the top bar of one of the pens and knotted it to the stout wood. He had made what looked like a noose, going by the Westerns. He had tested to see that it would tighten by grabbing the rope circle through which his head would go and yanking down hard. He thought it was the right length so if he dropped from the rail of the pen his neck would break from the drop and his feet wouldn't touch the ground.

But someone would have to find him. And probably that would be the Unthanks. Johnsey couldn't bear the thought of upsetting them like that. Himself was surely sixty-seven or eight and Herself was about the same. Would they be alive ten more years, or twenty? Wasn't he just a hardship to those lovely people, treading his big dirty boots in through their bakery each day, looking for his lunch, and plonking his fat arse down in their kitchen and slobbering all over their table? And to make their penance harder, he was now helping himself to further charities in the dinner and Sunday-lunch department. Everyone in the village knew he was a fat eejit, he had never really hurled properly, girls looked like they pitied him or they joined in when lads laughed at him. There must have been a great mix-up somewhere along the line with these big plans that Father Cotter does be on about. Surely with the universe as big as it was, God could allow himself a slip-up here or there. There was hardly a deputation of angels banging on His door shouting Hey, God, you forgot to give a justification for Johnsey Cunliffe's existence, he's below scratching his hole like a fool, waiting for a reason not to do away with himself!

★ ★ ★

It would be summer soon enough. The Unthanks always went somewhere thousands of miles away like Sligo or one of those quare counties for weeks on end to a niece who was married to a right bigshot by all accounts and they had a rake of kids and a huge big house. They would leave Kitty Whelan or Bridie Mac running the bakery. That would put paid to Johnsey's lunchtimes of ease and luxury for a while. His loneliness then would be *absolute*. That meant complete, total.

Something had to give before summer. How would he manage being so lonesome *and* dealing with the types of situation that would require more spoken words and more complicated ways of stringing them together than he was capable of? Maybe he would take his holidays from the co-op at the same time as the Unthanks and close up the gate and the house and pull the blinds and the curtains and let on to be gone away himself? Sure, for all Packie Collins or any of his sneery relations knew, he was doing a strong line with a girl from the city and they were gone away sunning themselves out foreign. Or they were going to a *ski resort*! Imagine, there were fellas his age less than two miles away that had actually done that kind of thing! Headed off in a jet to a ski resort in some faraway country full of glamour with a girl and flew down snowy mountains and drank liquor with foreign names and rode the girl all night and come home engaged to be married and the whole place would talk about how brilliant it was and tell them they were great. Lads who had been in his class in school led that kind of a life. Imagine.

★ ★ ★

Johnsey wondered was there a way to get away from this earth cleanly, to just disappear one day and have no fuss about it nor hassle for anyone. A lad from above around Gurtabogle fecked off to Australia a few years ago and went missing out there and sure that was that, really. What was anyone going to do, go and turn every stone in Australia looking for him? Australia was so big it was a *continent*.

The same lad had been in Johnsey's class in primary school. They went on a school tour once, as far as Lahinch. That time, they were all still pally enough. Eugene Penrose hadn't yet decided to lash out against the world in general and Johnsey in particular. The Gurtabogle lad, Mikey Kennedy was his name, went out

58

swimming with the rest. While they were all fooling near the water's edge, splashing each other and throwing mud and running away screaming at the sight of a jellyfish, Kennedy started swimming, straight out from the shore. Sir and Miss had given strict instructions on the way down to the beach that everyone was to stay near them, and to only swim parallel to the shore. PARALLEL TO THE SHORE! Ye *blackguards*.

But Kennedy swam straight out and it was nearly too late before Miss spotted him and screeched at Sir who was chasing lads around with a jellyfish *actually in his hand* and he dropped the jellyfish and let a roar out of him that Kennedy was to get back *this instant*. Kennedy was a small black bobbing ball by then. You couldn't see his arms any more, but they must have still been working hard because he was getting farther and farther away towards the horizon. He was swimming into the sun. Everyone stopped messing and shouting and stood with their hands shielding their eyes looking out towards the shiny horizon after little Mikey Kennedy and the only sound was Sir roaring for him to come back, come back, for God's sake. Then a lifeguard dashed past and nearly knocked Sir over and Miss put her two hands over her face and said Sweet Jesus over and over again. Afterwards, Johnsey heard another lifeguard saying how it was lucky Sean had been on duty; he was a junior champion swimmer, the lad had got so far out it mightn't have been as clean a rescue if anyone other than

Sean had been there.

When Sean the Lifeguard made it back to the shallows and waded in to the shore with Kennedy in his big freckly arms, he flung him down on the sand and Kennedy just lay there crying. Sir asked him what in the *fuck* he meant by that stunt. Kennedy just said I don't know, Sir, and kept on crying and coughing, and the whole class stood around him in an embarrassed circle and stared, as shocked at Sir's *fuck* as at Kennedy's near thing. Then Miss put a towel around his little shoulders and gave him a hug and a kiss and told him it was all right and more than one boy wished then that *they'd* been the one to strike out for the horizon.

Ten years later, that same lad, Mikey Kennedy from Gurtabogle, flew off to Australia and went missing out there and was never seen again.

⋆ ⋆ ⋆

Time drips by. It never flies, really. Time only ever flies in the last few minutes of a match when the team you're rooting for are a point behind. And that's reversed if they're a point ahead. A townie lad in school once told how if you tied a lad up so he couldn't move and dripped water on his head, for a finish he'd go mad and each drip would feel to him like a hammer blow. The Chinese used to do it to their enemies long ago. Johnsey only half believed it then but he fully believed it now. He could feel each second drip from the clock above the press and splash down on his head. You had to trick your mind sometimes, to distract it from the drips, or they'd become hammer blows and you'd end up like one of them Chinese lads. You could pretend you were Nicky English scoring before him in '89 if you were abroad in the yard beating a *sliotar* off of a wall. You could pretend to be heading off on a trip across America in your shining Ford Mustang if you were farting about up and down the yard in Mother's old Fiesta. You could imagine you were a secret agent, deep undercover, disguised as a mysterious young bachelor, living alone and awaiting further instructions from HQ.

If you were feeling especially lonesome, and just sitting in the kitchen, say, and you let it out through the gate because you weren't concentrating properly on keeping a rein on it, your mind could have a fine old wander about for itself. If it got too much leeway, it could start trying to point things out that you could otherwise kind of gloss over or shove away into the dark spaces. It could start calculating the amount of time you spent on your own now that Daddy *and* Mother were gone, and the time to come to be spent alone if you lived a full life. Three score and ten, you were allowed by God. You could go a good bit over that, even. Daddy hadn't gotten his allotted time at all. The likes of poor Dwyer and that young lad of the Clancys got nowhere near it. It could remind you of how it had seemed life was only temporarily suspended when Mother was alive and would maybe get underway again in some shape or form as soon as the dark weather brightened, but now it seemed to be at a full stop. It could start adding up the number of lunches and dinners the Unthanks had given you, and you never once put your hand into your pocket, except to have a secret scratch of your balls. It could start reminding you about all the different ways in which you didn't match or measure up to the other fellas your age: you had nare a woman, nor a hope in hell of getting one; your only friends were two elderly people you had only inherited as friends; you'd been terrorized by a little prick called Eugene Penrose since you were a child; you couldn't walk home through the village without shitting in your pants in fear of him. You were not able to hold a normal conversation, your mind would remind you. Nobody wanted to talk to you, anyway. People that did, it was only because they felt they had to. It could remind you that you were a useless, orphaned spastic. It could make the deep pool in the river or the crossbeam in the slatted house seem like sweet salvation from the miserable torment of just being.

Your mind could become separated from you altogether. Johnsey was starting to see this now. You could end up abroad in the yard, chasing it around like a madman if you were not careful. It could become free from you quite easily and fly off down its own path. There were a few evenings where he had sat watching television and had all of a shot realized he had been just sitting there, and there was nothing only blankness about him; he hadn't been asleep or awake, he couldn't remember what he had been looking at on the telly, and once there was a long line of dribble hanging from his chin.

★ ★ ★

On the way home from the mart Daddy often used tell him about some of the old boys they had met that day who lived alone in the real and true back of beyond, their little cottages stuck to the side of the mountain and not a soul coming near them from one end of the year to the next. They'd slosh around in shite up to their knees in Wellington boots that had holes in them; they'd be black with the dirt always and would only have the one pants for weekdays and one for Sundays and their weekday pants would be ready to walk off them and away down the boreen. They'd have a name for each beast in their herd. They'd be right fond of those beasts. That was the way for many a small farmer who never married. Often you'd have two old brothers farming the same land and living like two old smelly peas in a half-destroyed pod of a house. Or you might have an auld wan that had never married and she would serve as a wife to her bachelor brother. Not in *every* way, surely. Quare things went on, though; he knew this from things he overheard.

One day, below in the co-op, shortly after Packie had taken him on as a *general assistant*, he had heard a big, red-faced lady talking to two men who were so interested in what she was saying, they were bent nearly double to get their hairy old ears closer to her flapping mouth. It

63

seemed the guards had taken a man called Formley from some quare townland in the back of beyonds Johnsey hadn't heard of away from his farm and family. His children had been *put into care*. The same family were not sorry to see him go, by the red-faced lady's account. His wife was dead but years. He had a daughter and two sons. She had been expecting, the daughter, and she only sixteen. The father was either her own father or one of the brothers. This man Formley had taken care of this bit of trouble, with a rope and a broken broom handle. The girl's insides were ripped to shreds. Her wounds got infected, her blood turned bad, and she was near to death when the guards arrived. Her child was found wrapped in a sheet on the ground near the septic tank. The guards were only called because the man had drank what whiskey was in it after his little operation and went mad about the place and fired off his shotgun and his youngest lad made a dash for the house of a neighbour who had summoned help.

They were the bits Johnsey had heard. Putting those bits together in a way that made sense was impossible. Were they all going at her, her father who was given the job by God of protecting her from harm, and her brothers as well? The whole rest of that day, that girl's suffering rested heavily in the centre of his mind. For a finish, he felt a sort of a weakness from thinking about it, a sickness in his stomach and a woozy feeling in his head, and he had to sit down on a pile of fertilizer bags and try and collect himself before Packie spotted him. Imagine, that jagged, broken broom handle entering her and piercing a little unborn baby and yanking it out, dead and bloody into this world.

Probably it would have been a monster anyway, the red-faced lady said. A *monster?* Surely be to God nothing with a baby's pure, unblemished soul could be a monster? But there was something about that in Johnsey's mind, something about fathers and daughters and brothers and sisters riding each other. *Incest,* it was called. If they made a baby it could be a retarded freak or have two heads or worse. But then, Adam and Eve's children must have done something like that to make the human race grow, and then it must have happened again when only Noah and his family were spared from the Great Flood. Or did God let Noah's sons' wives live too? Even then, there would have been first cousins riding. And Johnsey had heard that used as an explanation for more serious cases of gamminess or spastication: Yerra sure, weren't his parents first cousins?

★ ★ ★

For a man to be lonely, Johnsey knew, he did not need to be alone. People often took his hand and shook it and held on to it in the co-op, and stood reminiscing about one or both of his parents while his face burned and his other hand searched vainly for somewhere to put itself. You could be lonely even then, with a person actually standing right there in front of you, clutching your hand, saying things to you. A couple of

65

days, it seemed there was a *queue* of such people. Some of them had been at the funeral but thought it would be nice to have another go at shaking his hand and telling him he was after getting an awful time of it, and he was to call up any time, any time at all, they were *always* at home. Their door was *always* open. He'd like to see their faces if he actually strolled in through their door. Hello! Here I am, as invited! I'll ate me dinner now and have a cut of tart after it and a couple of bottles of stout and maybe have a good feel of that young lady over there, is that yer *daughter*, bejaysus she's a fine girl now, and I'll be on my way again! Woo-hoo!

They'd have a hairy conniption if he as much as set foot in their yards. Why did people go around saying things they didn't mean?

★　★　★

There was an old fella, his name was Quigley, used to live away over the road and down past the small bridge and on past the weir, over towards the stud farm owned by the Black Protestant Shires. The Shires had *old* money. That was more valuable than new money. This old fella had a small bit of land tucked up to the side of the Shires's walled-off ranch. He was a wild-looking man, with great clumps of hair sticking out from the side of his head and from under his cap. He wore a greatcoat tied with baling twine all year round, and Wellington boots coated with slime that he fermented all over his yard. On purpose, just to spite the Proddies,

Daddy used to say, good Catholic shite. When Johnsey was small that man of the Quigleys would cycle on up the road past their gate, and he'd always have a big cheery wave, and he'd go all the way out as far as Clonvourneen. Every single evening without fail, come rain, hail, sunshine or storm, he'd make that trip. He'd pedal his old creaky, squeaky, rusty pushbike all those miles out and all those hard miles home to visit an old uncle of his who was being subvented in the nursing home out there. He'd sit beyond with him and they'd have a chat and a brandy and he'd fix his old uncle up for the night and see that he was comfortable. Daddy said he was only doing it so that when the old uncle died, he'd leave him everything. For a finish, after all the thousands of miles cycled, and all the elements braved, the man died before his uncle. The fucker outlasted him.

Daddy always said that that man did what he did out of *avarice*, and Johnsey believed that then, because when Daddy said a thing it was invariably true. But now, Johnsey was not so sure. Maybe he did it to have somewhere warm to sit of an evening, with someone familiar to look at and be silent beside in comfort. Maybe he knew that was worth more than a farm of land or a big pile of second-hand money, covered in the dirty prints of other men's hands.

April

Daddy would leave the cattle out of the slatted house at the start of April. They'd think they were going to be milked and they'd queue up like fools at the milking-parlour door. Then Mother and Daddy and Johnsey would hunt them up the yard towards the long acre and they'd be looking back with their big scared eyes as much as to say Are ye sure? Are we *really* allowed out here? Mother would say Look at the auld eejits, go on, ye auld dotes, and the three of them would watch as one brave auld campaigner would mosey off in to the grass and the rest would get courage from her and follow on. Friesians are pure gentle auld crathurs. If they were Limousins, Daddy would say, they'd trample you to get to the field. They'd knock the feckin wall!

* * *

Dermot McDermott called up to the house at the start of that April. It was a Monday evening. Johnsey brought him in to the kitchen. When you came in through the front porch and into the hall, you could turn left into the kitchen or right into the front room, the good room. There was no way that curly prick was tramping his dirty rotten boots in around Mother's good room that she fussed over for so many years and was

68

forever tightening up for fear anyone would call. He'd probably sneer to himself at the pinkness and frilliness of the cushions and the lacy yokes Mother put over the backs of the couch and armchairs. And the picture in pride of place on the wall above the fireplace of Daddy and Mother and Johnsey, taken when he was a small boy by a *professional* photographer inside in town, with his hair all combed back and his good-wear clothes on him. Dermot McDermott would probably have a great time describing it all to his bigshot people. But then, they'd probably all done their fair share of nosing about the place when Mother and Daddy died. They'd surely been in the stream of people that had flowed in and out to offer their condolences and pay their respects. Johnsey couldn't properly remember; those two sets of days were like dreams you only have a half a hold of when you wake.

What kind of dealings would he be made part of? Would he have to make a decision or give permission for something or talk about the lease on the land or agree to a right of way or some such adult thing that Daddy or Paddy Rourke or even Mother would be able to sort out with a wave of a hand and a few small words? When they spoke that way the unaccustomed listener could go away thinking nothing much had been said, but in those brief conversations not a word was wasted, each utterance contained a world of meaning. Dermot McDermott had never said a *bad* word to Johnsey — he had never said many words to Johnsey at all — it was a way that he had of not looking at you, or looking around while he was talking to you, like you were not quite deserving of his attention, so he would examine the countryside all about until you were gone away and had stopped usurping his precious time. At least he wouldn't be bullshitting about calling up and calling down and doors being always open and other such lies people think are truths while they're saying them.

This must be the way those fellas in wars felt before the little prick of an officer blew his old whistle and they had to climb up over the top of the trench and run at the enemy. Here was he feeling that same terrible fear over a *conversation*. The thought of talking to a fella his own age from over the road was the same as running towards a load of mad Germans who were firing machine guns at you! Imagine that. He'd have been shot as a coward for sure. Maybe running and firing a gun and trying to avoid being blown to bits were easier things than talking, though. It was surely less complicated. If you survived, you probably wouldn't be lying awake that night thinking did I look like a spastic running through that field of barbed wire? Are all the other soldiers laughing at me?

★　★　★

Dermot McDermott wanted to know could he buy out the land.

Johnsey was caught on the hop rightly. All he could do was stand there with his mouth

70

hanging open, staring at Dermot McDermott like an unadulterated gom, while the words hopped around his brain like them balls in the Lotto. Dermot McDermott told how their milk quota was going to be doubled shortly and they wanted to be sure of the land, like. How's it he couldn't just tell him to go on away and have a shite for himself, there was no one going buying out his father's land? For a finish he told Dermot McDermott that he didn't know, he'd have to ask. He'd have to *ask*! Imagine saying that. Who would you have to ask? Dermot McDermott's eyes darted left and right and his bushy eyebrows furrowed together, as if searching for this phantom that needed to be consulted about the land. Maybe the ghost of Mother or Daddy would appear from the fireplace and say Go on out in the yard now, son, we'll take care of this little bit of business. They would probably be better at this dead than he was alive.

★　★　★

Why couldn't cancer have minded its own business about Daddy? Why couldn't Mother have toughed it out without him another while? Wasn't it a solid fright to say that a chap could be left high and dry, with neither dinner nor bed made for him, and having to have dealings with sneaky neighbours over land and what have you? It was a fright to God and that's for sure. Every word he had said he could hear back, clear as day, echoing around his thick skull, making him want to just turn off the lights and cover his head and never set foot in sunlight again. *I'll have to ask.* Oh. Mother. Of. God.

Having a conversation like that, out of the blue, when a chap wouldn't be prepared, could take it out of you. You had to let the thoughts about it just come and go by themselves. There was no point forcing yourself to think things or not to think things. You could do yourself damage trying to work things out too quick. There was no way he could sell the land. It wasn't his, anyway. Uncle Michael who fell and was killed beyond in London, Granddad, Daddy, the IRA great-uncles — they were all still knocking about the place, Johnsey knew, keeping an eye. He was the end of their line, imagine. They must be browned off over that. Selling the land would be the last straw. You could be so much of a letdown and get left away with it by virtue of being a gom and not having full use of all of your faculties. To sell their land and give the rest of his born days sitting on his hole looking at the television, landless as well as friendless, that would beat all for badness.

★ ★ ★

Johnsey looked around the kitchen. It wasn't the last word in cleanliness, but he had had it tightened up fairly okay. Dermot McDermott couldn't be going back to his witchy old mother and telling her it was like a pigsty beyond, sure he wasn't half capable of managing by himself. Imagine, though, if he was a bad yoke and he sold up to hell. Imagine the stuff he could buy!

72

But there was money in a bank account belonging to Mother that belonged to him now. It was what she was paid by the insurance when Daddy died. There was also a big pile of money in the Credit Union below in the village belonging to him that Mother had put away over years. One of the aunties had told him all about it and how to go about getting it if he needed it, but what would he need it for? All that stuff to do with money and deeds and what have you was safely above in Daddy's little office and there it could stay until some space in his brain could be freed up for such matters. Anyway, you couldn't sell what wasn't yours, and the land would never really be his. He could live on it and walk across it and for years he'd helped farm it, or at least he'd traipsed around behind Daddy and did his best not to balls anything up, but he was not *of* it the way that Daddy was. If he took money to let the land fall from Cunliffe hands he'd be a traitor and a blackguard.

Daddy had often talked about money as though it was only a nuisance of a thing that you had to pay heed to only the odd time. Mother berated him over his attitude — it was *lacks-a-daisy-kel*. You wouldn't see the McDermotts or the Flynns or the Creamers beyond not minding their money. Or them Grogans below in the village, they grigged Mother no end and they having the grocery and the post office and the drapery and the hardware and the undertakers and the bar and the bed and breakfast and the garage and a farm of land and three or four more farms of land left to them (that people *knew*

73

about!) and the board of the Bank of Ireland couldn't so much as fart without Herbert Grogan's permission, he had so much money stuffed into their accounts and he claiming expenses, imagine, every time he scratched himself because all the goms around the place kept voting him back onto the County Council and do you think for one second that Herbert Grogan would do in a month the work your father would do in a day? He would in his eye! He had cuteness coming out of his ears, though, that was the difference. He'd put legs under hens for you, that chap.

Why, Mother would demand, would a man who worked so hard have so little store in the bit of money his work made him? Daddy used to lay blocks as well as farming the land. He took what them auld builders gave with no argument. He never thought to up his rates. Was it unmanly to want to be paid properly for the pain in your back or the sweat of your brow? He had tried to show Johnsey how to lay blocks, but he just wasn't *tasty*. You had to be quare tasty to excel in that line of work. Your plumb line had to be right, your hand sure with the mortarboard, your eye sharp so that you sat the block just right. Johnsey could hold a block in one hand fine, but he couldn't lay his mortar at the same time. Or he could lay mortar but not if the other hand had to do something else. For a finish Daddy would grab the board and the block off of him and tell him go on away and tidy up, they were going. If Johnsey looked back, as a rule, he'd be shaking his head.

Mother often said to him to mind his bit of a job, it would stand to him. You had to have a job to get a job, she said. If you hadn't really the *aptitude* for farming or for a professional career, you had to be punctual and conscientious and hard-working. You had to make the most of what you had. What had Johnsey? A big thick head into which travelled only black thoughts of how much he hated being here on this earth alone and a big pair of hands that were good at nothing only lifting bags of fertilizer and spuds and a heart that was cowardly and broken. How could you get past all that and into a place of reason and happiness and ease? Could your mind ever be at peace when you had to be afraid every minute of the next bark from the old dog Packie or the next smart remark or jostle or put-down or kick from Eugene Penrose? How could you call yourself a man when you came from a family of men who would face down the devil himself and you unable to face down a cross old bollix or a little smirking squirt?

★ ★ ★

The next day came wild and windy. A breeze that would skin you made short work of the softness that had been in it the last few days as it whipped around the high walls of the front gate, doing its level best to push him back inside. Nobody had told this wind Hey calm down, it's nearly summer. It battled him the whole way to the village and then, just as he reached the old pump, the heavens opened and an almighty shower of icy rain landed on him. He had the jacket without a hood, of course. And you couldn't be seen with an umbrel unless you were a woman or very old. If he bowled up the street holding an umbrel it would surely be grabbed off of him and he'd be tormented for being a queer.

Packie thought it was great sport that he landed in frozen and drowned wet. He laughed and shook his head as much as to say you could expect no more from a fat eejit only to be caught out in the shower and told him go stand in front of the Dimplex. The Dimplex was no great shakes in the drying-off department: the co-op was like a huge damp cave and the Dimplex was old and tired and probably as sick of Packie giving out about it as Johnsey was. Before the warm air had even settled on his sodden legs, Packie got sick of his own charity and Johnsey was sent packing to the yard. He threw a poncho at him at least. Johnsey slipped it over his head and its plasticky skin made him feel colder again.

Packie wanted space cleared abroad in the yard for a big delivery. It was a full day's work if not two days' were you to do a right clean job. Some places had forklifts; Packie's co-op had a big donkey called Johnsey Cunliffe. The delivery would be arriving at four, so tough — four was the deadline for a cleared yard. There were rakes of pallets to be moved one by one to the side wall; there were bags and bags of feed under a huge canvas to be uncovered and brought inside and space to be made for them; there were racks of shovels and forks and garden implements that Packie had bought long ago in some quare figary

76

he had gotten thinking people would travel out from town to buy gardening tools in a small country co-op. Packie thought he'd be the height of fashion. Even Johnsey could clearly see that Packie Collins would never again be the height of fashion. Maybe he was a big draw one time, when your family having the co-op meant you were a fierce big deal.

The great delivery came a half an hour late. Lucky thing too, as the clearing was only barely finished when the lorry rumbled up the road and squeaked and puffed to a stop outside the gates of the yard. Packie was like an old biddy at a jumble sale; flapping around and trying to act like he didn't give a damn what was coming, but you could see the redness creeping up his neck and his eyes bulging out of his cranky old head a bit farther than usual. The lorry was full of timber, two-by-four and four-by-four and what have you in long, clean planks.

The next day, just before lunch, two huge blue skips were dropped from two lorries that had great swinging arms and chains for the job of picking things up and leaving them back down. These skips were to be filled with the wooden racks that Packie had once stocked with plants and flowers in the days of high fashion and with all the other unused, unwanted, out-of-date and broken things that lived in Packie's yard. Johnsey half expected to be told to climb in himself, such was the mercilessness of Packie's purge. Packie even took an axe to the racks himself but his glasses fell off after the first few swings and he cursed and spat and soon rolled the sleeves of his smock coat down and retreated back inside behind his counter.

The next delivery to come was of concrete blocks. They were deposited in the yard by a ferrety-looking fella who had a forklift that had been stuck to the back of his lorry. He moved quickly and placed pallets of blocks side by side along the back wall with vicious exactness. He made Johnsey nervous. Neither he nor the yard were used to such frantic noise and activity. Packie was rubbing his hands together a lot. Even old Biddy, Packie's hairy-faced wife, arrived for a look at the big consignment, all lined up now like a rank of giant, grey, alien soldiers. She looked like a cat that had been fed too well. Johnsey could imagine her licking cream off of her whiskers.

Then came a delivery of bags of cement. The cement had to be placed in dryness for fear that it would start to set. Johnsey could hardly believe the massive, dead weight of the bags. He had pains in his legs and arms after it. His back was okay, though; Packie had insisted on showing him a video one time about how to lift heavy things without blackguarding your spine. You had to put all the weight on your legs and hold the burden in close to your body.

★ ★ ★

Eugene Penrose and the dole boys were lying in wait at the pump that day. They had set up a new camp, it seemed, closer again to the co-op so that they would not have to wait as long in the evenings for him. It must be thirsty work, tormenting your fellow man: they were all drinking cans of Harp. Johnsey wondered what it would be like to give a whole day drinking cans of Harp. Would it be great craic? It must be great sport being on the dole because Eugene and his pals were always laughing. There was a new lad with them today — he was a townie, Johnsey could see: he had his tracksuit pants tucked into his socks. Those townie boys always did that. You would see gangs of them inside around the market if you travelled in with Daddy, all with their tracksuit legs inside in their socks. Maybe it was so their tracksuit legs wouldn't get caught in anything when they were running away from the guards.

Eugene Penrose said Here's auld Cutehole Cunliffe with his big farm of land worth millions and a grand job as well and the whole fuckin parish on the dole. See this fella, lads? He has millions, boys, and he goes in every day to the co-op to be a fuckin gimp for Packie Collins!

The townie boy was harder-looking than the other three. He had one of them sharp, ratty faces that a lot of townie boys had, and there were three blue birds tattooed on his neck. They were flying up towards his ear. His head was skinned. He was looking at Johnsey and smiling madly like a child would look at an animal in the zoo that he'd never seen before. He had to look at his new friends to be sure that they were seeing the same thing; that he was really real, this fat, soft-looking farmer's son, who had just bowled up the road to provide him with sport.

Johnsey didn't think the whole parish was on the dole. Plenty of lads had trades, more had jobs inside in town, and plenty more had fecked off altogether and were professional people above in Dublin and other big places. It was the lads that had run straight from the school gate to the meat-factory door that were all on the dole now. The likes of that place was never going to last, Daddy said. You could only rely on them Arabs for so long to want all that beef, and there were rakes of countries queuing up to sell it to them cheaper.

Eugene Penrose said When you get all them millions for that farm above, you'll still be below getting rode up the hole by Packie Collins, I suppose.

Why did he keep on about these millions? Daddy always said the farm was worth feck all. Fellas who weren't from land, of course, would always be going around saying every farmer was a millionaire. Mother had often said that. Eugene Penrose was standing in front of Johnsey now, and his breath was warm and stale on his face. Johnsey could see little red lines zigzagging across his eyes. He was breathing hard through his nose and his watery snout was quivering like that of a young bull. Johnsey half-expected him to start raking the ground with his foot.

He was moving closer so that their noses would soon be nearly touching and Johnsey could feel that familiar lightness between his legs. Dwyer said once it was nature's way of minding a man's goolies — that lightening, crawling feeling was your balls retreating

80

upwards for shelter from violence, so that if a fella drew a kick at you you'd still be able to perform with your wife and so the survival of mankind was assured. Lads were forever getting lamped in the balls millions of years ago by all accounts, so nature had to try and do something about it for fear there wouldn't be a sperm left that could swim straight. Eugene Penrose was saying Won't you? Ha? Auld cutehole farmer.

His face was kind of twisted, his lips were pulled back from his teeth and his eyebrows had arranged themselves in a V shape that made his eyes look even madder. He was wicked-looking. Why was it Johnsey always had to get the brunt of this wickedness?

Some fellas, if confronted with the likes of Eugene Penrose's big auld snotty beak, would draw back their arm and swing a fist into his puss so fast he'd be out for the count before he knew what had hit him. Or they'd butt him right on the snout with their foreheads. He'd seen a lad one time, a lad younger than Johnsey himself, pulling the helmet off of one of the Toom boys during a hurling match and boxing the face off of him. Johnsey had never been able to draw a kick or a swipe. There was something always stopped him. Probably it was that big yellow streak that had somehow, against all the grains of nature and breeding, found its way into his soul. What power did a yellow streak have? It could paralyse a man's arm and leg and though his head would tell him lash out, that streak of yellow would make him cringe and draw inwards and turn into a hedgehog, a little shivering ball

81

in front of the wheels of a car.

Eugene Penrose was saying Look at the cut of you, you fat fool. What do you be at above on that farm, anyway? Do you get your hole off a different sheep every night? The townie boy hooted. The trick was to just keep trying to walk to his left or right and if he pushed you back to just kind of lean against the push so that you kept making forward progress, and eventually, with the help of God, he'd tire of the game and you'd get past him. Today he was pushing harder, though, and with the third push Johnsey was knocked to the ground. The wind was knocked out of him. His legs had lost any will to help him out. He looked up the road; there was nobody. He looked to his left; the dole boys were putting their cans down on the wall around the pump. He knew they were going to give him a hiding.

He could tell the two with Eugene Penrose weren't as interested in this carry on as their leader, but they would go through with it out of fear of him. The townie was a different story. He was smiling ear to ear and laughing in a screechy, high-pitched way and was clearly planning on planting one of his dirty runners in some part of Johnsey's body. *Tackies* them boys call them. All he could do now was curl up in a ball and cover his head as best he could. The last time something like this had happened to him was shortly after the meat factory had closed down and Eugene Penrose had kicked him in the stomach one day so hard he couldn't breathe for ages and after he stood up he felt so weak he nearly fell again and he got sick on the side of the road just before he reached home. When he went inside, Mother told him he was white as a ghost. He said he wasn't feeling great and she ran him a bath and gave him soup and said if he was the same in the morning she would ring Packie Collins for him and tell him he was sick and would not be coming to work. The memory of Mother's tenderness tore at his soul.

★ ★ ★

When Johnsey was small he'd had the same dream over and over again for one whole summer. It was the summer that Bonesy Donnell died and his sawmill was closed up and locked. Bonesy had always frightened children, not on purpose, but just by being humped and crooked and having arms that were longer than was natural and hands that had thick hair on the backs of them and a kind of a mad smile that made his kindness seem more like a desire to eat you without salt. A few nights Daddy had had to come in to him, and once he lifted him gently from his bed and carried him down the hallway to their room and Mother kissed him and tucked him in between them for the night. That only happened the once, though, that he could remember.

In the dream he would be walking past the high gate of solid wood at the sawmill yard. It would always be locked, with a big padlock that you could see was unbreakable. He would hear noises behind the gate, like someone was using the big circular saw inside but not properly — he could hear a noise like someone was trying to saw through something less regularly shaped and *wetter* than wood. Then the screaming noise of the metal being sawed would change to a human screaming as the padlock burst in two and flew off in different directions and the sawmill-yard gate swung inwards and he would be rooted to the ground, just standing there, unable to move as a humped black shape grew from the shadows and then he would see that the black shape had lifted the circular saw and the whole bench from the ground and the screaming blade would be coming straight at him and he would wake with his breath gone from his lungs and his covers would be on the ground and his sheet would be wet with sweat and once his pyjamas were soggy with pee.

★   ★   ★

When Johnsey came to he could not see. He was still on the ground; he could feel that his hand was in a puddle of water and he could smell rain and something else that was damp and dirty, like there was a wet dog somewhere near him. There was a taste of metal in his mouth. He could just make out a pulsing light and someone was saying You're okay, good man, in a soft voice and then he felt himself being lifted and then doors slammed and an engine started and he slipped away. He had the dream again, and this time the black shape had a face and it was the townie fella's face and it was roaring out of the sawmill yard at him that he was a *faggot* and a *fat cunt* and even Eugene Penrose was a bit shocked-looking and wasn't joining in any more and was saying Ah fuck it, come on, leave him to fuck.

★ ★ ★

The next time he woke he was in a bed. It wasn't his own bed, it was harder and there were metal bars either side of him. They were cold to the touch. He could smell something like Dettol mixed with shit. He was fairly sure his eyes were open, but still he couldn't see. Then a young woman's voice, soft and soothing, said Did you wake up? and called him *love* and said Don't worry now, you'll be fine, the doctor will be in to you in a few minutes. Then she said some words that he didn't understand and she click-clacked away into the distance.

He spent a few minutes trying to have thoughts one after the other instead of all together. He was in hospital, obviously. He had a clear memory of being knocked down on his arse by Eugene Penrose. There had been a townie lad with Eugene and the boys and Johnsey had a memory of the townie lad descending on him in a whirling cloud of punches and kicks, but it was like he was looking at what happened through the glass of a toilet window. He remembered thinking this fella was going to murder him and he'd be on the news and they'd show the pump with a yellow tape all around it and a little *bangharda* minding the murder scene and there'd be a bunch of flowers left by the

85

Unthanks and they'd interview random villagers who would say Sure he never harmed anyone, his parents were lovely people, he always kept himself to himself, isn't it a fright to God that this could happen in our lovely village?

There were little pinpoints of light flashing on and off and that was all he could see. They must have kicked him in the eyes. Could you kick a man's eyes out of his head? It didn't seem likely. Still, Mother always said them townies were fit for anything. He remembered feeling like something was exploding in his head every time that ratty lad's runner connected with him. He should have covered himself up better. But he remembered that feeling of letting go and falling apart that came over him and it must have been after that that his defences crumbled altogether.

He was in some stew now: no mother or father to mind him and he as blind as a stone. Would he be able to manage to get a cartridge into Daddy's shotgun even? Knowing his luck he'd miss his useless brain and blow half of his face off and he'd spend the rest of his born days being a blind monster, sitting on a chair somewhere with people lining up to scare themselves by looking at him. Some would be brave and they'd come up right close and poke him. Others would only be able to look at him through their fingers — the women mostly. Children would cry and try to run away, but parents would make them look and they'd say Now, look at what's waiting to come for you if you're bold, he's the bogeyman and he eats bold children. And he'd sit there, unseeing, with one

86

old Cyclops eye left and a mad, useless eyeball rolling around inside in it.

★ ★ ★

If those neighbours of Daddy's relations were able to give themselves over to the devil to get their hands on land that wasn't theirs, why couldn't Johnsey do the same now to get up out of this bed and be a different man? He could make a solemn pact that on his death he'd travel straight to hell and give eternity in scorching fires. In return he'd be transformed into a man who could rise up out of this coward's cradle, sight restored, with muscles all over him like that vampire fella with the blonde girlfriend and he'd slap the nurse's arse as he left in his cool grey suit and sunglasses and they'd all stand there shocked to see this handsome hero stride out of the hospital and one woman at least would faint away at the sight of him. God had deserted him, so why shouldn't he switch sides? The devil might give him a better run of it.

That was the thing about the devil, though, Johnsey knew: he would promise you the world and every blue and green and growing thing in it and give nothing but more torment. Didn't he try that old trick with Our Lord and he famished and parched in the desert? Lies is the devil's currency. You wouldn't catch Jesus making deals like that crowd beyond who had all the land they wanted but no immortal souls to call their own and the gates of heaven barred to them.

*   *   *

The Nurse with the Lovely Voice whispered back in to say the doctor was very busy and would visit him on his normal rounds this evening. It was two now. He'd had woeful bad luck in the eye department, by the Lovely Voice's account. His poor old eyes had had two separate strokes of bad luck: Eugene and the townie and the other two apes had split his left eye right open. A surgeon had stitched it back up. And his retina in his other eye had been knocked from its rightful place and the same surgeon took that eye right out of his head and fixed it up and struck it back in but it wouldn't be fully right again for a good few weeks; the upshot was he would not be blind forever and wasn't that great news and sure he supposed it was.

The other big news, said the Lovely Voice, was that his right arm was broken clean in two and was in a plaster cast and so were three of his ribs but they would have to heal themselves without the help of a cast. He had *massive bruising* on his legs and back. When he was admitted his head had been swollen but there was no damage to his brain (no surprise there, he nearly said, there wasn't much to be damaged) and the swelling was nearly fully gone down now and a *cat scan* had been done and from there Johnsey was lost again, swimming against a tide of big words.

He had one big question he needed to ask but he was damned if he was going to go embarrassing the owner of that lovely voice. How was he going to go to the jacks? And just as the question presented itself in front of his blind eyes, she answered it, as if she could read his mangled thoughts — a *cat eater* had been inserted into him and that would drain his bladder. It was all cats in this place. Now that she mentioned it, something was not quite right down there. His mickey felt like it had more going on than usual; it wasn't quite sore, but it wasn't the height of comfort either. What about it? Just as long as this cat eater didn't bite.

What about having a shite? He lay there and hoped she could see this question floating around as well. She could begod. The Lovely Voice told him he was to tell her when he wanted to *move his bowels* and she would give him a hand. How in God's name was the Lovely Voice going to help *move his bowels*? Was there not a cat eater they could assign that horrible duty to? She took his good hand and guided it back and up towards his head to what felt like a big knob and told him he was to press that when he needed a nurse. She would be going off duty soon but there would always be someone there for him. And then there was the sound of a rattling trolley and a singsong townie voice said Hello love, will you have chicken or beef or pasta salad for your di-nnerrr, and he said Beef, thanks, and the Lovely Voice said she would give him a hand with it if she was still here, sometimes they did this ward first because they were near the kitchen. Johnsey prayed to that treacherous God that they would. If he was going to be spoonfed like a big mangled baby, his mortification may as well be accompanied by the Lovely Voice.

It would soothe you, that voice. You could just lie there, listening, and lose yourself in it. You could pick it out from away down the corridor, and follow its approach in laughs and greetings and delicious words being flung carelessly here and there. And that's what Johnsey did for the rest of that long April: he listened for the Lovely Voice and waited for the light to come back. Like the flowers abroad in the gardens, pushing up through the darkness towards the sun.

Some flower he was.

May

May is always lovely, no matter what. You're meant to seal the borders of your land against *piseogs* on May Eve by sprinkling holy water on the ditches and praying to Our Lady for protection from badness. May was Daddy's mother's name. She was a famous beauty. She could make the stones laugh, too. May was Daddy's favourite month. Was that because it was the month for which his mother was named? Maybe it was because it was a month of grace and beauty and smells that could make your heart feel like it was going to burst. Daddy wasn't inclined to explain himself, though; it was his favourite month and that was all there was to it.

There was a May altar abroad in the corridor outside his room. The Lovely Voice told him about it. If you *saw* the one that put it up, you know, and she decorating Our Lady's feet with daffodils as much as to say there's a pair of us in it! She'll be looking for a halo of her own next. Silly slapper!

★　★　★

Some things is easy do, when you have no choice in the world but to do them. Like shiteing into a bedpan, in front of a nurse. Or having bits of you felt and examined and talked about by doctors in quare words that don't sound like normal English. Thinking about it, it seemed as though it was always that way. It's easy have things happen to you. All you have to do is exist. Making things happen back is the hard thing. Like words: they're grand to listen to from other people, and when they're words spoken by the Lovely Voice they're like a 99 with a flake in the middle of summer, but it's fair harder to try to arrange them for yourself. There's no pleasure in listening to yourself, that's for sure, only hardship in the knowing of your own stupidity.

The faithful Unthanks came nearly every day to see him. Himself would shuffle around the bed and Herself would tell him sit down and he would huff through his nose like he was annoyed. She would say to Johnsey You poor pet, and Himself would huff again as if in agreement. One day, when he was gone to the jacks or the shop or somewhere, she leaned in closer to Johnsey's face so that he could smell perfume and bread and Mass off of her and she said Himself never stops talking about it, you know, you getting bet up like that. It's after upsetting him more than anything ever upset him before in all our lives.

All Johnsey could do was nod.

She said he charged off bald-headed over to the Ashdown Road like a bull, and into the Villas, that first night you were here in the hospital, and he nearly went in the front window of the Penroses's house and there was four or five of them there, you know, but he saw no fear he was so cross and he effed and blinded and cursed every one of them and told young Penrose if he so much as looked at you sideways ever again it'd be the last thing he ever did, but that crowd only laughed at him.

There was a stinging behind the bandages. Salt on his wounds. Himself came back and she leaned away again. He was huffing more now, after the stairs.

Will you eat a Twix, Johnsey?

I will. Thanks.

A Twix was easy ate.

★ ★ ★

The Guards had come, of course. A fella with a beard in a shirt and tie — a *detective* no less — and a skinny lad in a uniform, the Lovely Voice had told him. That was shortly after he had come round. They had asked him what happened and he had told them he didn't remember too much except the bit of pushing and shoving and he was knocked and a fella he didn't know with birds on his neck had taken an awful dislike to him, it seemed. The guards laughed a bit at that. They told him don't worry, they'd come back when he had his sight back and he could look at a photo and *formally identify* the bird-neck lad, but he had been questioned already and so had his three mates and they had been told in no uncertain terms that they were to stay local. Johnsey told the guards he'd rather they fucked off to be honest and they laughed again and Johnsey nearly felt good about himself for a second or two.

There was a doctor who was a specialist in eyes. He came in most days for a look under his bandages and he'd let a *hmm* or two out of him and he'd go away again about his business. He sounded foreign. His name was Doctor *Fostiwaw* or *Fastibaw* or something quare like that. One day, the Lovely Voice told Johnsey that she just called him Doctor *Frostyballs* and he laughed so much he could feel his cat eater nearly slipping out. A real card, Daddy would have called her. What would he do when he could see again? When his eyes were right and there were no more worries about his swelled head or his bruised kidneys or his cracked arm, he'd surely be given the road. He wouldn't be left malinger in this bed, that was for sure. And there'd be no Lovely Voice breezing in and out of the rooms of his cold old house.

★ ★ ★

Packie Collins came in to inspect the patient in his bed and Johnsey imagined him with his face scrunched and his nose all wrinkled up and he looking down through it like a fella would look at something that was stuck to the bottom of his shoe. He wanted to know what in the Jaysus was he at, fighting on the street like that? Johnsey didn't answer him. He there and then made a decision: he would never again darken the co-op door. He'd minded his little job long enough. That must be the secret to making decisions — don't think about them beforehand, just do whatever makes you feel most like a proper man.

94

Like Daddy in the mart deciding on a beast or your man in *ER* deciding to leap up on the operating table and ram his hand down a lad's throat to save his life.

Packie said he'd had to get a little lad in to give him a digout. Things was gone fierce busy. There was going to be a lot of building starting up around and the co-op yard was going to be a sort of a *staging area* for the builders. A little foreign lad, he is. A good little worker now, mind you. Packie must have gotten over the powerful aversion he had to foreigners. Johnsey said You may hold on to him for good, Packie, I won't be back to you any more, and the minute he had the words said he started to disbelieve that he had really said them; he listened for an echo of them in his brain and waited to feel them settling back down on his face like the fine mist you'd feel off of that waterfall beside the hotel where Mother's cousin got married that time when he was a small boy. He started to think he hadn't said them at all when Packie said Well! Well, well, well. Well, that's the solid Jaysus finest! Oh begod, don't worry at all! Sure I was only being foolish thinking Master Cunliffe would appreciate my holding his post open while he recovered from his injuries!

It was easier be brave when you couldn't see your bravery's result. You could probably punch a lad in the face a lot quicker if you hadn't to see his eyes while you did it. He could hear Packie take a step back. He was *taken aback*. That wasn't just a saying, then. He'd be below in the co-op afterwards reading Johnsey to all who'd

95

listen. He'd label him a blackguard and an ingrate and he'd have a wounded puss on him, but inwardly he'd be rejoicing. You hadn't to pay foreigners as much — everyone knew that. Packie said Well, well a few more times, and then he was gone.

Well, well.

Good luck so. You auld bollix.

★ ★ ★

Aunty Theresa paraded in at three- or four-day intervals, giving out stink to all before her. She dragged her husband in with her half the time and poor little mousy Aunty Nonie the spinster the other half. Daddy used to call Frank *that poor fucker* and Mother would let on to be insulted on Theresa's behalf but she'd smile in spite of herself. Daddy used to say about Aunty Theresa that you had to have a business in town and a farm outside town before she'd look at you. There wasn't many measured up to Theresa's test of respectability. Even Our Lord Himself had only the carpentry business and no land. Signs on the only ones who'd be pals with Him when He walked this earth were the fishermen and prostitutes and lepers. The likes of Johnsey and his terrible predicaments were sent as a trial for poor Theresa. It was a penance for the few old sins she'd committed, to have a nephew like Johnsey making a solid show of her by getting into such common scrapes. God knows they weren't much to write home about, them few auld sins she committed that were

96

being held against her still, but some are given a bigger burden than others and all we can do is suffer on and not give out.

Aunty Theresa said he had their hearts broke. They expected him every Sunday but he was below with them Unthanks constantly. He hardly looked at them above at Mass! He was all that was left of their lovely Sarah and *now* look at the cut of him! Uncle Frank or Aunty Nonie would tell her *whisht* but you couldn't whisht that one up. It was just too much; it was *too much to bear*, all this constant heartache. One evening she was in full flow about how awful it was about Johnsey fighting with bowsies and what have you and in walked Doctor Frostyballs and she all of a sudden sounded like one of those horsy Protestant ones whose lips don't fit down fully over their big front teeth who come in to the co-op for feed now and again. She said Hellooo Dawk-tur, but old Frostyballs only gave his usual few *hmms* and shagged off fine and quick. He hadn't time for mad Irish aunties to be wedging their tongues up his hole. Aunty Theresa said he'd be a very high *caste* now, you know, in India.

He would I suppose, said poor old Frank.

*　★　★　★*

There was only one other bed in the room. It was a *semi-private* room. He was in the VHI, and he hadn't even known it. That meant you got special treatment because some crowd above in Dublin or somewhere would foot the bill. You

97

would get the best of stuff. Imagine that: his mother still had to sort things out for him and she dead and gone. She wouldn't have liked him to be in a big old ward, anyway; you wouldn't know what kind of quare-hawks would be in it, Mother would have said.

One time, when Daddy was bad, he'd been rushed in and given new blood and afterwards they'd wheeled him into a big ward full of auld fellas so they could keep an eye on him. Mother and Johnsey were left stay with him for fear he'd die without company, and a nurse pulled a plastic curtain around them. There was no room available, only the big old ward, stinking of old men and piss and shit and whatever dark medicines were used to try to hold Death at bay. Daddy was dead to the world, drugged to the solid eyeballs. Halfway through the night an auld fella took a figary and leapt out of his bed and threw their curtain back and stood there looking in at the three of them and he without a tooth that was ever known and his bit of white hair standing straight up on his head and shining eyes on him like a greyhound inside in a trap and his old wrinkly mickey peeping out through his pyjamas. Mother hopped out of her chair and made a grab for the old rogue but he sidestepped her and he was gone in between the wall and the side of Daddy's bed and next thing wasn't he going at Daddy's face and Mother was trying to drag him off and a nurse and an orderly ran in and got him back into his own bed and they strapped him to it for a finish and through the whole thing Johnsey had just sat there like an

98

imbecile, looking out of his mouth.

Some help you were, Mother said.

It turned out the old boy was gone mad for the want of a drink. He had never gone a day without a few glasses of stout and a whiskey chaser or two, maybe. That was enough to send a man mad for the want of it, if that man had given fifty years without going without.

★　★　★

A procession of roommates were wheeled in and deposited in the other bed in Johnsey's *semi-private* room. None of them went at him like that old campaigner had gone at Daddy, thanks be to God. He saw none of them; he only got a few blurred seconds of sight in the evenings when Doctor Frostyballs was lifting his bandages and doing his *hmm*-ing. All you could make out in those few seconds were a pair of brown eyes and a hairy brown nose. He wished the Lovely Voice could do the bandages so he could see *her* eyes and nose instead. Doctor Frostyballs's touch was gentle. His *hmms* sounded kind. Johnsey felt a bit guilty for the jokes about him he shared with the Lovely Voice. Well, he listened and laughed anyway. He was a willing accomplice. Sometimes after he was gone she'd arrive on and start taking him off in a foreign accent and it was funnier than Brendan Grace. She would stand at the head of his bed to carry on her blackguarding. He could smell her: roses and medicine.

She'd say: I am reading your chart now. Hmm

99

. . . yes . . . hmm . . . I am seeing that you are not responding to my very brilliant doctoring . . . hmm . . . It seems to me as though there is only one course of action left open to us, young mister blind fellow . . . hmm . . . and that is to amputate your face! And he'd say how that'd be no harm, anyway, and she'd say Aw, you have a *lovely* face.

They must train them to tell lads things like that who are in bits inside in bed to make them feel better. She was fair handy at it, though. You could nearly let yourself think she really thought you had a lovely face. Imagine his old puss after getting kicked to bits, as if it wasn't offensive enough to start out with. She was probably hardened to ugliness, having to look at old wrinkly arses and bedpans full of shite for a living.

★ ★ ★

Mumbly Dave arrived towards the end of Johnsey's third week as a blind invalid. He wasn't quiet, but it was all the one — you couldn't make out a word he was saying, only mumble, mumble, mumble. The Lovely Voice said he'd had a mother and a father of a fall off of a ladder and he'd landed on his face on a fence. His ribs were all broken like Johnsey's, his teeth were nearly all gone and he had a broken arm like Johnsey. He had a broken leg, too. His face was swollen and smashed, and his eyes were closed tight from the swelling. They had had to put wire into his jaw to hold it together.

I have a fine pair on my hands now, the Lovely Voice said the first day Mumbly Dave was wheeled in. A fine pair of smashed bumpkins! You could be as bold as you wanted when you had a voice that could send the devil back to heaven. He wasn't called Mumbly Dave straight away — it took the Lovely Voice nearly half a day to come up with that. *Smashed bumpkins, two blind mice, thing one and thing two*, she gave a whole morning in and out with a new title each time for the pair of them. Johnsey could hear his new compatriot forcing short gusts of air down through his nose each time she breezed through and dished out a little morsel; the painful laughter of a man who's beaten and broken-ribbed. Johnsey wasn't fond of this new development: he didn't want to share the Lovely Voice's attentions with this clumsy ladder-faller-offer. He wished they'd wheel him away again and bring back a silent geriatric.

He had felt like he was getting special treatment. It was out of pity, he knew, but she never made that obvious. You could fool yourself into believing you were the only one whose ear she whispered evil jokes into about the ward sister or the old boy in the other bed or Doctor Frostyballs or Aunty Theresa or whoever came within range of her wit. He didn't want to have to share the Lovely Voice, especially not now that he was nearly finished on the painkillers and his eyes were healing up the finest and his bruised kidneys had come round a bit and he'd very soon be given the high road home. He could picture the newcomer: a big builder lad, probably, with muscles and blond hair and a jaw on him like Desperate Dan. Even with his broken face and nare a tooth that was known, that lad would most likely put Johnsey in the ha'penny place.

★ ★ ★

The Unthanks knew him well, of course. Ah, Dave, is it yourself, you got an awful hop, we nearly heard the bang below in the bakery, ha ha ha, is this fella looking after you, sure you're both in the same boat, talk about the blind leading the blind, ha ha ha! Herself had to tell him be quiet and come away and leave the man alone. She had to take him in hand every now and again. Mumbly Dave didn't seem to mind. His mumbles back to Himself sounded happy enough. Some people loved the bit of attention.

There was *big news*. The whole village had it. Herself had got it off the ICA. They had all rang her one by one, each thinking they would be first with the news. Himself had got it above at Mass that morning. Himself went every morning, to Mass. He went to confession too, at the required intervals. Religiously, he went. Was there any other way to go to confession? What did he tell the priest? Surely he had to make sins up. Wouldn't that in itself be a sin, to be told at the next confession? A fine, eternal circle of sinning and contrition.

Mumbly Dave was doing awful mumbling beyond, as if to encourage the speedier telling of this big news. And the Lovely Voice would be on in a second as well; he could hear her abroad in the corridor, laughing as usual. You could easily judge the direction she was heading. She pushed a wave of fun and devilment before her and left a trail of it in her wake. She would hear the big news too, if the Unthanks ever got around to telling it.

The council inside in town had been to-ing and fro-ing and fighting and arguing for years and had finally made a big decision. A load of the land to the west of the village had been *rezoned*. That meant that instead of being simply fields of grass for tilling or grazing, the land the council had marked out with a red marker and put on display on a map for all to see inside in the civic offices was now land on which houses, shops, hotels and what have you could be built. That land included all of Daddy's, and nearly all the Creamers', and half of Paddy Rourke's and a bit of the McDermotts'.

They were as excited as wasps around an open bottle of Fanta about this big news, so it seemed only polite to try to join in. He nodded a good few times and said Begod that's great and Oh really and waved his good hand about a bit. He preferred when the Unthanks were their usual selves; this much talk out of them, and the two of them talking over each other, and the speed they were talking at — it wasn't right somehow. It could make you feel a bit nervous, like if a grand, quiet old dog was asleep by the fire at your feet and all of a shot, for no reason you could fathom, leapt up and began barking and going mad about the place.

Anyway, this apparently was the best thing that could ever happen to any small village, according to everyone bar the few usual moaners who'd object to their nose to spite their face. It would be a new lease of life for the place. Even those who had been gone but years might reconsider their positions in life and return, if there was something to return to in the line of a job doing all this building and what have you. Sure hadn't a pile of young lads only left recently, sure they'd turn the planes around if they heard this news. They'd nearly jump overboard off of the boat and swim back. There had been fierce speculation for the last few months, but it was as though people were afraid to jinx it by saying it out as a certainty. Once it's used right, now, that's the important thing. People will have to keep a close eye on applications going in and protest if they think something is going to go up that will do more harm than good — the likes of discos or fast-food shops or what have you, with any luck they will be excluded from the plans.

★ ★ ★

Packie Collins's yard and it full to bursting with blocks and timber and bags of cement. Dermot McDermott's offer to buy the land. Eugene Penrose's talk of Johnsey's millions. They had all been a mile and a half ahead of the Unthanks. Mother had always maintained that the auld sneaky ones always had news before anybody. Some, the cuter ones, would keep it to themselves and more would go around telling all they knew to anyone who'd listen. They'd spread news that wasn't even news yet. If there was nothing to tell, they'd make something up.

Like the time years ago the whole place had it that Paddy Rourke had belted the head off of Kathleen and she only after getting a black eye from a rejected calf she was bottle-feeding who butted her by accident. Once a thing was said, it could never be unsaid. Paddy was blackened after that in many minds. Some people believed what they were told regardless of who it was doing the telling and wouldn't be waiting around for hard evidence. The Unthanks weren't that way; this was officially true and therefore could be discussed as fact. You couldn't be ruining it for them by telling them that it didn't matter one shite if Our Lord Himself wanted to buy land off of Johnsey to build houses and hotels and shops on — Johnsey's land did not belong to Johnsey — it was not his to sell or to allow people to build things upon.

* * *

Mumbly Dave was more inclined to talk properly after a few days. They put a hinge in that auld wire in his jaw and gave him a new mouth of temporary false teeth in case the world missed something important out of him. After a small bit of practice, the mumbling was replaced by a non-stop flow of words. Johnsey had envied him his wired-shut jaw; there was no pressure on a man with a wired-shut jaw to be saying things to people. How well it was his eyes had been

105

broken and not his jaw. Then he could see the owner of the Lovely Voice instead of just imagining her and he wouldn't have to be trying to think of things to say back to her. Not even being kicked in the head could go right for him.

Mumbly Dave felt no such pressure in the talking department. In fact, talking seemed to be his way of releasing pressure. It was as though thousands of words were squashed up together inside in his head and couldn't wait to rush out of his mouth like a crowd out of the tunnel under the stand below in Semple Stadium after a Munster final. He thought it was a great big laugh that neither of them could see a screed in front of them. Mumbly Dave would say, I used to see no evil, speak no evil, now I only see no evil, ha ha ha! Hey, did you hear that, youssir, I said I used to . . .

He was all talk about the big news about the rezoning of the land. He wanted to know how many brown envelopes Johnsey had left inside in the civic offices, hoo hoo hoo. He wanted to know was Johnsey related to Oliver Cunliffe beyond in Latteragh, Oh are you not and Oh sure your father was Jackie, I knew him, he used to hurl with my father, sure they played Junior B until they were gone fifty, ha ha ha, they were tough yokes, Oh that was your mother so who died not long ago, sorry for your trouble, go on anyway, how much did you leave inside with that shower of crooks?

Was it you got the hiding off of Eugene Penrose and that fella from town and those other two apes? Penrose got an awful fright, you know.

106

He nearly shat himself apparently, when your man went to town on you. He doesn't know who he's mixing with, there. That lad is deadly dangerous. He's a pure knacker. He wore a pool cue off of one of the Comerfords and you know how tough them boyos are. Penrose is like a child with a new toy whenever a bigger knacker than him turns up. Do you work below in the co-op? Oh ya, I was thinking. You get dog's abuse there some days off of Penrose. I seen him at it a few times. And the other two fools with him. If Penrose opened his mouth you'd see their four cod eyes looking out at you, they're so far up his hole.

Begod Packie Collins wasn't long about replacing you! That feckin Polish lad was in like a fly on shit; I'll tell you one thing, you can't turn your back on those boys, they'd take the eye out of your head, I can't wait till this swelling goes down and I can open my feckin eyes, I'd say that nurse one with the nice voice is flaking, hoo hoo, hey youssir, I said I can't wait till this swelling goes down and I can open my feckin eyes, I'd say that nurse wan is flaking, I can't wait to get a good look at her, whoo boy I could sure do with a ride, ha ha ha, sure she sounds like she's gorgeous but we have to be prepared for an awful shock, she could have a face like a bag of hammers, ha ha ha, sure any port in a storm, maybe we're as well off if she's a right manky-looking yoke, not to be lying here with two horns on us every time she walks in, hey, how does that work with these tubes in our mickeys, anyway? Have you a tube in your mickey too? Isn't that an awful liberty? I don't know about you, boss, but them nurses can take as many liberties as they want with *my* mickey, ha ha ha ha ha!

★   ★   ★

Mumbly Dave made the Lovely Voice laugh. That was the thing about Mumbly Dave that really tormented Johnsey. How well he had to go and fall off his ladder and break his stupid face. How well he couldn't have broken his neck instead. How well they couldn't have left that old clamp on him another while. He was full of old sugary shite, that Mumbly Dave. Sure, he was a gas character. Ha ha fucking ha. How could he have a new joke or bit of smartness ready *every single time* the Lovely Voice came near them? You'd be heartsick, pretending to laugh. If he didn't hear a laugh out of you, he'd say the same stupid thing over again, only louder. He'd wear you out, so he would. If this was the alternative to loneliness, he'd sooner be lonesome forever. People could be quare hard work. He'd never known that before.

Another thing about Mumbly Dave was he kept *farting*. Johnsey had a pain in his stomach most days from trying *not* to let off. He had his arsecheeks clamped shut half the time. It had gotten to the stage where the farts didn't even bother trying to escape any more; they got as far as his hole and turned back. Then they'd be all knocking around his insides and fighting with each other for space. It couldn't be good for a man having all this pressure building up inside. Anything was better than filling a room with fumes, though, and having the Lovely Voice or one of the other nurses walking into a stinking cloud. Mumbly Dave thought it was the height of craic. He'd let rip day and night and then for devilment he'd put the blame on Johnsey. Once or twice his great big smelly farts coincided with the Lovely Voice entering their room and just as she did the rotten fucker'd say Jaysus, Johnsey, you're a bad yoke, would you not try and hold it in and a lady in the room and then he'd *mar dhea* apologize on Johnsey's behalf, the dirty, rotten bastard! The Lovely Voice would laugh and say Don't worry, I've smelt worse, and there was nothing you could say then; you couldn't be denying the fart and sounding like a young fella in primary school. Then after she was gone Mumbly Dave would be woohoo-ing and laughing away to himself and saying Jaysus, youssir, I caught you a beaut, and all you could do was lie there and imagine yourself sneaking over to his bed in the night and ramming a stolen fork into his mouth with all your strength. That'd soften his cough.

Some days the Lovely Voice would come in and close the door to the corridor and sit down and she'd tell them Say nothing, Sister is on the warpath, I'm safe in here with the blindman buffs, God I'm knackered; so boys, any news? And Mumbly Dave would be out with something smart straight away like asking was she out the night before and was she up late or what and the two of them would take off laughing and it felt like they were ganging up on him and he hated Mumbly Dave more than he'd ever hated Eugene Penrose or Dermot McDermott or Packie Collins or the townie lad who'd kicked his face in or any of the cool lads who'd mocked him in school. Why did Mumbly Dave have to come along and wipe his eye? The Lovely Voice was *his* bit of pleasure; she used to have private jokes with *him*, it wasn't fair that the first proper woman to ever whisper in Johnsey's ear and send a bolt of electricity down his neck and along his arms and into his balls and down his legs as far as his toes was now being taken over by a big, fat, stupid bullshitter.

★ ★ ★

Johnsey and Mumbly Dave got their eyes back on the same day. Mumbly Dave woke up that morning and said Bejaysus you're uglier than I thought you'd be, hey I said you're even uglier than I thought you'd be, hey, hey, youssir, you're a sight for sore eyes, ha ha ha ha ha, and Johnsey could only lie there and look blindly in the direction of the guffawing donkey and think this is the end of it now, he'll take one look at her and fall in love with her and he'll carry her off like Richard Gere in that film where he's in the navy or something and he has a big fight with a black lad and takes off on a motorbike and into the factory where the good-looking wan is working and he'll pick her up like that in his arms and carry her off and all the other nurses and doctors and the few patients around the corridor will stop what they're doing and laugh and clap and cheer and Johnsey will be left here alone with the cranky old ward sister and his langer stuck to the side of his leg and his big baby tears queuing up behind his bandages.

Your swelling is gone right down, that's the anti-inflammatory, it takes the swelling right down, isn't it lucky you're on my ward; I give out all the best drugs, ha ha ha. Then Mumbly Dave, her new pet. Ha ha ha you're a gas ticket, bejaysus, I'll tell you one thing, though, the swelling is gone from my face but tis starting somewhere else ever since you walked in, ha ha ha. Then the Lovely Voice: You dirty fecker, ha ha ha, and she *mar dhea* giving out to him. He had some neck, that Mumbly Dave, he had some front, that fella, with that dirty talk out of him, and she laughing back at him, and wouldn't you think she'd tell him call a halt to the smut now, but thick ignorant fuckers always get ahead in life, Daddy always said that, and he was right. Then she was saying As for *you*, your bandages will come off today for good according to your chart, unless Doctor Frostyballs changes his mind, and he realized she was talking to him and he said Oh, oh, right, cripes that's great, and she was gone in a sweet breeze and there was no big laugh and joke for him the way there had been for Mumbly Dave.

I'll tell you one thing, youssir, she lives up to her voice, she's a fine thing, a bit over-endowed in the arse area but sure that's part of being Irish, ha ha ha! You'll see for yourself later on, anyway. Isn't that gas we're both finished with blindness on the same day? We were brothers in blindness there for a good while. It's grand, though, having a comrade like yourself. Whisht, here she's back, here she is, hello my flower, what have you for us? When are you taking off Johnsey-Come-Lately's bandages? It's lousy me being the only one having to put up with looking at a horrible mug all day, lucky you're in and out to relieve the horror for me, ha ha, wait till *he* has a look at *me* he'll want them bandages put back on quick smart, ha ha ha, make sure you're here when Doctor Frostyballs does the big reveal or he'll fall away in a faint, ha ha ha, like a baby chick thinks the first thing it sees is his mother, he'll be going for a suck off Doctor Frostyball's boob, ha ha ha, hey, youssir, did you hear that, I said . . .

★ ★ ★

Being blind wasn't so bad. When you knew it wasn't forever, especially. If it was for good, and you weren't bedbound, it would for sure be a bit awkward. But there was comfort in that darkness; you could let things carry on around you and there was no need to be thinking should I do this or go there or say that. All that business with the land now being *part of a very valuable land bank*, as the Unthanks said Martin Doherty the auctioneer called it the other day in the bakery, could be safely ignored while a man was blind and bedbound. The only anchor to this comfort he would have left once he had the full use of his eyes back would be the tube up his mickey, which would be surely yanked out once he was capable of jumping out of bed and making a piss by himself. Imagine your life being that much of a ball of shite that getting kicked to bits and going blind was the best thing that had ever happened you.

A different lady took away the cat eater. She called it a *cat ate her*. Maybe it had a different name because it was finished its job now. They had quare names for lots of yokes in hospitals, anyway. It didn't hurt coming out but it was sure as hell hurting now. It was after leaving an awful burning behind. She had tut-tutted a few times and held his mickey in her hand for a while longer than seemed strictly necessary. Then she tut-tutted again and asked him had he any pain and he said No, because it wasn't paining him too bad at that stage and he didn't want to be giving out about nothing. Then Doctor Frosty-balls came in and took away his eye bandages. His head felt wrong without them. The world looked wrong. He had imagined the room as a mini version of the ward they put Daddy in the night of the madman, but it was way newer-looking than that; if you took away the bits of machines beside the beds it could be a hotel room like the one he and Mother and Daddy had stayed in one time they had stayed above in Dublin after the All-Ireland and Daddy had got a bit merry and Mother had gave out but laughed at him too and a rake of people were in the bar of the hotel and they all sang 'Sliabh na mBan' and Mother had sat him up on her lap and she sang too and he had tried to sing it but he only knew the one or two lines and she had her arms tight around him and was rocking side to side with the rest and it was the best feeling he ever had before or since.

★ ★ ★

Doctor Frostyballs had brought a girl with him and she stood there smiling and took the bandages in a silver bowl and handed him a small bottle and he dripped a few drops into Johnsey's eyes and said Yes, it's good, things will be blurry for a while more, your pupils will be *di-lay-ted* for one hour then no more problem, you will see things floating in front of your eye, *that* will be forever, you will get used to them, if you see *flashes* you come right back to me. Then Doctor Frostyballs and the smiling girl went off about their business and all that was left was a load of blurred shapes and he lay back and tried to sleep and enjoy his last few unseeing moments before the world was back around him, clear as day and waiting for him to do something or say something for himself.

But the throbbing in his mickey kept him awake. He opened his eyes and sat up and made a tent out of the blankets that were over that area so nothing would touch off it. Something wasn't right with it. He could see grand again now. He chanced a look over at the quare fella and there he was, grinning back to his two ears, nothing like he had imagined: a small, baldy lad with eyes that looked like they had twinkly stars in them and big fat lips and the lips looked like they were

114

bursted in the middle and his whole face was black and blue and yellow like a bad spud you'd dig up and throw away and his arm was in a sling and his leg was up in a bigger sling that hung from what looked like a miniature crane and he nearly said Where's Dave until the little baldy lad started talking and he knew for sure.

Well hello there, youssir, did you decide to have a look at me at last, aren't we a fine pair of crocks, well at least we can have a gander around for ourselves now, and a read of the paper and a look at the telly and a few of them nurses would cheer you right up, but a few more would frighten the life out of you, one of them has a *tacher*, and I'll tell you one thing . . .

Then he was asking Johnsey was he all right and the room started to spin around and he got a feeling like the time he snuck two pint bottles of stout and a rusty old opener that no one would miss down to the willow tree one Christmas and drank the two of them off the head by himself and just before the stout and his dinner leapt back up from his stomach in an orange stream, the whole world had started to fly around in circles and all he could do was try to hang on and all he could do before the darkness came back was tell Mumbly Dave who wasn't a fine cut of a fella at all that his mickey was in an awful way and should he tell someone?

June

Daddy would always do the second cut of silage in June. You'd hear the tractor abroad in the long acre as you trudged off in the morning. The big schools inside in town would be closed but you'd still have a month to go. A *month*! The sun would never hang on that long. The summer would be gone before you were released from the misery of listening to the whoops and cries of the free from the dark, sweaty inside of the small-windowed classroom. How did Sir stay going? Surely he was as jealous as they were of the wild emptiness of school-less days.

Cast nare a clout till May is out. June and July, swim till you die. That's something Daddy used say at the beginning of June always. Shut up with that auld eejiting, Mother would say. Have you your bikini ready, Sally? Daddy would say back, and he'd wink over at Johnsey, and Mother would go red and try not to let him see how she was smiling behind her mask of temper.

His *you-ree-tra* had gotten infected. That was the thing inside his mickey. *Bacteria* had somehow found its way along the cat eater. Cat ate her. Cat et ur. Whatever the hell that yoke was called, it was quare handy when a man wasn't fully mobile but for a finish was proving to be a source of awful trouble. All he knew was he was only able to stay awake for minutes at a time and every time he came around he was

116

frozen with the cold but someone would say he was very hot and he would try to say he wasn't, he was perished, but he'd slip away again into a world of crazy dreams. He saw Mother and Daddy and the two of them were below at the bottom of a beautiful garden and he wanted to go down to them to ask how they were and was it nice being dead and he wanted to tell them how his life was like an empty bottle of red sauce, there was nothing in it and no point to it and you could stick your knife right in and root around forever but all you'd get was a small bit but never enough to make you happy and for feck's sake why wouldn't Mother buy a new bottle of sauce when the old one was finished, she'd never leave Daddy without his *brown* sauce, he'd be giving out stink saying Any brown sauce, Sally, because he nearly always called her Sally and he was the only one who ever did.

There was a big yoke beside him now and it frightened the life out of him the first time he saw it and there were two bags hanging off it with tubes coming out of him and the tubes were stuck in his arm. The first time he saw it, it looked like a big alien robot with bug eyes and he thought it was a dream and he tried to pull the wires out of his arms but an angel was beside him and there was bright light all around her and she told him it was a drip and it was putting medicine in him and he'd be fine and the angel had a lovely voice, just like the Lovely Voice and the angel *was* the Lovely Voice, of course, it made sense now, he wasn't dead and in heaven or hell or purgatory so, but this couldn't be far off heaven, floating about like this and seeing lovely angels with golden hair.

★   ★   ★

He was panned out after it. Jaysus you got an awful dose, youssir, Mumbly Dave told him, and you only days from getting out of here, you misfortune. It was hard to stay awake. The infection had left him very weak. He'd have to stay on another while. Misfortune? It was a huge stroke of luck. The Lovely Voice was now a lovely face and lovely hands and a lovely light-blue uniform that he thought would be white but then he realized he had kind of been imagining them ones that do be in the ads in the back of the *Sunday World* unknown to himself, dressed up as nurses, and the ad says things like *Sexy nurses on the line, waiting to give you your medicine* and there's a big long phone number and you can see nearly all their boobs and a bit of their knickers under their short white skirts and wasn't he an awful pervert to have been imagining the Lovely Voice in that way without even knowing he was doing it? If only she knew, she wouldn't be as gentle and kind to him and she wouldn't be in and out to check on him even when she wasn't really meant to be.

Siobhán, her name was. Imagine that, all these weeks, and he hadn't known. *Siobhán*. It was soft. It was easy, saying it. You could whisper it and it was like a breath, or a sigh. It was the most beautiful name. It nearly tasted sweet in his mouth.

Siobhán gave him great hop again now and seemed to have forgotten all about Mumbly Dave. She felt a bit responsible for his infection — she had been meant to be taking out that yoke every so often and changing it and watching for badness starting but she couldn't be remembering everything all the time, there wasn't half enough staff here, anyway, and if that fat cow of a sister asks make sure and tell her she was forever pulling and dragging and checking that all was well with cat eaters and cat ate hers and what have you. She was awfully sorry; he could see that clearly.

He would tell any lie for her but it wasn't really a sinful lie. It would be like telling the English officer that the boys had been tucked up in bed all night long when they'd really been abroad around the countryside shooting Black and Tans — it was a lie, but neither God nor man could ever hold it against you.

★　★　★

Siobhán said the old ward sister was an awful wagon, and a few of the other nurses were pure sly and were terrible licks and they'd stab you in the back as quick as look at you. They wouldn't do half the work she would do, but yet would be forever watching her and reporting back to Sister, and she knew why — it was because they were all the one with the nurse she was filling in for who was out on maternity leave and they wouldn't let her be seen to be as good as their friend. Mother would have called the likes of them *poisonous bitches*. Johnsey told Siobhán that, and she laughed. Then she did something you would as a rule only see happening in a soppy film: she put her hand on the side of his face and smiled down at him and he chanced looking straight into her eyes and it looked like fondness he saw there or maybe something beyond fondness; maybe she saw him in a way that no one else saw him — after all she could only judge him on what she had seen since he was carried in by the ambulance.

Maybe she had more regard for him than other girls would have because she had never seen him walking watery-eyed up through the village with Eugene Penrose pelting stones or scrunched-up cans at him or seen him getting kicked around the school bus or being set fire to and having his fiver swiped off of him on the way to the only disco he ever nearly went to. All she knew of him was that four yahoos had attacked him and he was in bits but never gave out and that he was a grand quiet chap who took his medicine and didn't moan or groan like some lads did. Hadn't she told him he was a great patient? Probably she would sooner a fella like Mumbly Dave, even though he was a handy-sized baldy lad with a belly like a beach ball. Mumbly Dave never stopped talking. Maybe she saw Johnsey as being a bit like Clint Eastwood. Clint Eastwood never said too much but bejaysus he sure was cool. James Bond wouldn't be the chattiest, either, but girls were forever trying to get off with him.

And besides saying he was a great patient,

120

which was not a thing you could go around boasting about because as far as he could see being a patient only involved lying down, she had paid him four compliments. He remembered her exact words and the way her voice sounded as she said them. They were the only compliments he had ever gotten from a girl who was not either related to him, in the ICA or Mrs Unthank. The first was about a week after he was brought in, when he was still very woozy and they were pumping him with stuff to stop pain. He distinctly remembered her saying he had lovely long eyelashes, just after Doctor Frostyballs had done his daily check and she was gently replacing his bandages. Then not long after that she was helping him to sit up and she was making a meal of it and he was starting to feel embarrassed when she said Oh you're a big lad, and he'd thought she meant he was fat. Then she stood away a bit and he got the feeling she was looking at him. He felt his face burning and that's when she delivered her second compliment: she said he was very well built. *Very well built.* Now! And she'd know, too, being in a line of work where she'd get to see an assortment of bodies and body parts. The third compliment had come just a few days ago, the day after his bandages had been removed. She had said You know you have the loveliest blue eyes. The loveliest blue eyes. Imagine that.

So, according to her, he was a grand, well-built chap with *the loveliest* blue eyes and grand long eyelashes. It was all old talk, of course; he wasn't going to be cock of the walk around the place thinking he was a fine thing or anything. Still, though, she didn't sound like she was only saying these things for the want of something to be saying. The fourth compliment was the best of all; it had a proper ring of truth about it, like it was something that made her feel a bit sad to say it, somehow, but she had to say it, but she couldn't be saying it too loud because it was maybe more than a nurse should be saying to a patient. She was in around, tightening things up about the place and she stopped all of a shot and turned and looked straight at him and he looked away too quickly for her not to know that he'd been watching her progress around the room like an old dog would look at a joint of beef that had just been taken from the oven and she said You're *really* sweet. Do you know that?

That was one of the big drawbacks with a girl saying nice things to you: you felt you kind of had to respond in some way. What could you say, though? Thanks? That would sound like you knew this good thing about yourself already and fully accepted the fact. That would make you a bighead. You couldn't be refusing the compliment either as then it could seem as though you were fishing for further compliments by making the other person argue with you. You could try being cool and nod and kind of let on you didn't care what they thought but that would most likely just look plain ignorant. Best thing was just to go red and mumble, which really was the only response he was capable of, anyway. Going red and mumbling, all things considered, was the perfect way to react when someone said something nice about you.

*　*　*

By the time Johnsey's fever broke Mumbly Dave was on his feet regularly and mooching about and tormenting poor souls up and down the ward. Siobhán arrived in one day, just after Dave headed off to see who could he inflict himself on. I'll just have a look at you, love, and see are you all ready for road. Road meant home. Home meant back to nothing, no company but his own thoughts and they'd start to turn on him again before long. No more Siobhán of the Lovely Voice. No more Mumbly Dave, who was the best friend Johnsey had ever had if he was to be brutal honest with himself. He was unnatural annoying, that man, but yet Johnsey couldn't imagine his own bedroom at home, with only a blank wall to his left and no little fat baldy fella spouting shite non-stop.

Siobhán had her hand on his mickey. She was looking over his head and up towards where Our Lady was perched on a little shelf, surveying the room and all in it. Johnsey could see a bit of the strap of her bra where her nurse's shirt had shifted slightly on her shoulder. It was black, and there were little lacy bits along the length of it. The bit of flesh that he could see yielding slightly under the bra strap's pressure was lovely and brown and freckled. Had she been sunbathing, he wondered? Girls loved that old craic by all accounts. It wouldn't stand to you in the long run, though, according to a wan on telly. You'd end up with a *melon omagh*. The sun was a sight for bringing out freckles. Those freckles were beautiful beyond any words Johnsey knew. She wasn't saying anything. Then her eyes came down from the statue's height and met his own.

Hmm, she went. Or *Mmm*, the way a woman in a film might if she tasted something lovely like a chocolate, or if a big muscley lad was kissing her neck trying to get off with her. Imagine, a girl was holding *his* lad and saying *Mmm!* This was one to file away for future reference. You could nearly fool yourself into thinking there was a purpose beyond the medicinal to her explorations.

She still wasn't saying anything and had made no attempt to move back his sheet to have a look underneath at his ravaged tackle. Probably these trained nurses could tell all by touch alone. An old John Thomas like his was all in a day's work, like a lump of rump to a butcher or a concrete block to a builder. Any second now she'd say all was well with his private parts, sorry again about that old infection, you're good to go, good luck, go on, there's more need this bed. But instead her hand moved up slightly along his lad and the little fella started to throw a few shapes. He felt his cheeks burn with shame. She'd think him a pervert. She'd let on not to notice his hardening but she'd rush off and scrub her hand and tell the other nurses what a dirty yoke he was and they'd all be wide-eyed and horrified and then they'd all look at one another and cover their mouths and break down and roar laughing at

124

him. Why wasn't she wearing a glove, anyway? Her cold hand moved down again and his skin was pulled back a little. Things were getting out of hand in her hand, but she didn't seem to notice; she was just looking at him but there was nothing in her blue eyes or on her lips to say what she was thinking. She seemed to be concentrating hard on something that was in her mind.

Suddenly she asked How does that feel? Her voice gave him a shock. He gasped out a *Fine*. Good, she said and stayed looking distant and thoughtful. He tried his damnedest to tear his eyes from that black bra strap. He feared he'd relapse into blindness from the effort. Was she wearing black knickers as well? The thought was out of the traps and running at full tilt towards his crotch before he could stop it and she seemed to sense this; she squeezed a little bit and her hand began to move up and down in an easy rhythm. The sheet across her forearm rose and fell no more than ten times before oh stars above oh mother of all that's holy oh oh oh, his eyes squeezed themselves closed and his heels dug into the mattress and his hands gripped two fistfuls of sheet as the hot, sticky fluid pumped and jumped and rushed in a flooding river out of him all over her hand and the bed and his leg.

July

No school in July. You could give every day knocking about the farm with Daddy. Or if he was right busy or had to go off laying blocks, you could stay in the kitchen and Mother would allow you sit up on the worktop and watch her baking, or you could walk over across the river field and see could you spot a rabbit or a hedgehog along by the ditches or maybe even a diving kingfisher. The sun didn't *always* split the stones, but even if it rained it was never cold and the earth would steam after it and you could even swim while it rained and you could kind of know then how the wild animals felt, being free.

Daddy would bring Johnsey to the Munster final, and Paddy Rourke would go with them as a rule. If it was on in Cork, they'd stop at the hotel in Mitchelstown on the way down for their breakfast. They always did a beautiful fry in that hotel. One time Daddy was going mad looking for more toast, but the little waitress must have gone off on her break or something, so Daddy bowled into the kitchen to make his own toast to hell and Johnsey was scared in case he got into trouble and Paddy shook his head and said Daddy was a madman and a few minutes later he came running back out with a big plate of toast and a load more rashers and a big fat wan behind him waving a wooden spoon *mar dhea* she was awful cross with him, but she was

126

laughing and Paddy and Johnsey roared laughing too and there were a few more there in Tipp jerseys and they all cheered and it was a pure howl.

The Pecker Dunne would always be busking below outside the stadium with a big pile of wild-looking children and Daddy was mad about him and he'd always put money in their box and salute the Pecker and the Pecker would salute him back and it wasn't everyone got a salute off of the legendary Pecker Dunne and Johnsey would be pure proud. If they beat Cork in the Munster final, Daddy would be as high as a kite on the way home. He'd shout Woo-hoo boys, we have Cork bet and the hay saved. Now we have a proper summer!

It's easy be happy in July.

★　★　★

You could nearly call him a man of the world now. He kind of knew what it was like to have a pal to talk to. Only kind of, because he had never returned Dave's warmth and they had never really had conversations; it was more a case of Dave never shutting up talking and Johnsey being forced to listen to him all day and into the night. Johnsey was a *captive audience* Daddy would have said. He couldn't help finding the bollix funny at times, though. And he did seem worried about Johnsey the time of the infection and the hot fever. Maybe if Dave hadn't been so smart and forward with Siobhán Johnsey would have given him more hop.

127

He knew now what it was like to be in love. One-way, hopeless love, he knew, but still love. They'd had a stand-in teacher one time inside in the Tech, a little blonde lady straight from university. She was a *fine thing* all the townie boys said, and they gave many a break time over to discussions of her body and how she was definitely gagging for it and how you could definitely see her nipples pointing out through her blouse and her bra and that was a sure sign she was mad for riding. Johnsey admired their brave talk, but secretly he preferred her pale-green eyes to any other part of her and the soft sound of her voice. She read out this poem in class one time. Johnsey never forgot what it was called: *The Dong With The Luminous Nose*. It was about a woeful ugly creature called The Dong who was head over heels in love with a beautiful woman who could never return his love. His love for her was *un-re-quit-ed*. Miss had written the word on the blackboard and underlined it twice and Johnsey had not forgotten the spelling nor its meaning. *Unrequited*. Not returned, not given back.

The whole class stayed quiet for that whole long poem and afterwards, instead of guffaws and smart comments, there was only a strange sort of silence, like some kind of desperate sickness had befallen lads who only a few minutes previously had been full of the joys of spring. He was one of the thickest lads in that class, but even Johnsey knew what she was at, that little blonde lady from the university, that shining angel among all the dirty devils: she was

128

telling them all they were only a shower of lovesick *dongs* and she knew full well they talked about her fanny and how she was panting for sex but she also knew each one of them was some way in love with her and they could sail away in their little boats and drown themselves in a sea of longing for all she cared; she'd never return their stupid, sweaty love. It was *unrequited*.

And he knew now what it was like to have somebody besides himself or that doctor that checks small boys' balls put their hand on him. There surely wasn't *too* much more a man could need to experience to consider himself worldly. The townie boys used to boast regularly about having gotten handjobs off of girls from the convent at lunchtime below in the castle demesne. Whenever a lad came in with this news it would cause a great stir. Some would be wide-eyed and want every detail, more would look sulky and roll their eyes and tell the boaster to go way out of that, he was bullshitting. One day a lad from Pearse Park arrived back from lunch claiming to have had the lad nearly tore off him by a wan from the convent and all were goggle-eyed at his story about how she had grabbed it near the top and yanked down and he roared out of him and she was awful put out over the aspersions he cast over her abilities and vowed not to leave him near her any more. The place was in stitches and the fella with the injured mickey was cock of the walk for days after, with fellas wanting to know how was his langer.

Dwyer had told him long ago that if you sat on

129

your hand for long enough the blood would stop flowing through it and it would go pure dead. If you could manage to close the fingers of that dead hand around your mickey it would feel for all the world like someone else was touching you. Johnsey had tried it, but no matter how long he sat on his hand, it never went dead enough so that he was able to fool himself. Dwyer used to have a great imagination, though. Maybe he could convince himself more easily. How's ever, he was one up on Dwyer now, that was for sure.

★ ★ ★

Uncle Frank drove him home from the hospital. It was the fourth of July. That's Independence Day for the Yanks. They goes mad beyond on this day, by all accounts, celebrating their routing of the dirty English. How come the Irish didn't do that? Didn't we beat the fuckers out as well? Bruce Springsteen had a great song about being born on this day. Frank threw an odd eye over at Johnsey's bag. You haven't much stuff, he said. Johnsey told him he only had the few bits the Unthanks had collected from the house and brought to the hospital. You'll be a while adjusting now to being on your own. Would you not stay with us a while? Teasie would love it.

Teasie. It nearly made her sound kind. She would in her hole love it, Johnsey felt like saying, but she *would* love to be telling all the biddies in the ICA and above at Mass how she was killed looking after the imbecile nephew and they'd tell her she was a saint and when her time came the

130

gates would swing wide for her for she'd have her penance well and truly done and she'd be left stroll straight in past smiling Saint Peter to sit at Our Lord's table.

The Unthanks were waiting in the yard for him. Johnsey could nearly feel the wave of relief breaking over Frank and splashing about the car. Good luck now and mind yourself. Grand, thanks, Frank. He fairly high-tailed it out of there. Poor old Frank, his life was made up of doing one thing after another that he didn't want to do. He probably would have loved to hear Johnsey's story about lovely Siobhán the sexy angel nurse and the black bra strap and the way she smiled after he exploded all over the place and gave two wipes and all the stickiness was magically gone and then leaned over and kissed him on the lips for a second and winked like a wan that would be on the telly late at night trying to make you ring a dirty phone line and sure a fella could hardly really still consider himself a *virgin* after all that had happened. And even still it probably wasn't enough of an affront to the Church to warrant his feeling guilty if he was to meet Father Cotter. There was no rule, as far as he knew, about handjobs before marriage.

See you soon, she had said, and he had not seen her again. How soon, he wondered? As soon as hell freezes over, you great ape. You big auld dong with a luminous nose. Don't be codding yourself.

★ ★ ★

After he had a fine lunch ate of juicy chops and floury potatoes and the Unthanks had finished fussing and were gone away, the warmth he'd had in his belly ever since the handjob and the kiss and the big manly hug he'd gotten off Mumbly Dave before he left and the promise to see him soon from Siobhán and the promise of going for a few pints at the weekend with Dave started to cool and fade away, like a dream that you really try to remember, but it just breaks up and floats off out of your mind and you can try to snatch it back but it's like trying to grab a hold of thin air. It probably wasn't real, any of it. Siobhán probably did what she did out of pure sympathy: she knew he had no hope of ever getting a woman to touch him. Nurses cared about people as a rule; she probably said Feck it, he's had a horn since he first clapped eyes on me, he's no trouble, really, the poor God-help-us, he didn't whinge about the infected mickey, I'll do him a turn to hell. For all Johnsey knew it was standard practice for nurses to relieve male patients in that way, just as they helped you empty your bladder and your bowel. Although surely to God Mumbly Dave would have loudly forecasted such pleasures. And that Mumbly Dave was a *plámáser* of the highest order; he probably invited everyone he met to go for a few pints. Anyway, he'd go through you, the auld talk out of him and the way he'd smirk behind Siobhán's back and make dirty gestures and then he'd be all auld froth to her face and you'd love to slap the puss off of him.

He was starting to feel the pain in his body

that the doctor had warned him about, behind his eyes and down the side of his face and in his ribs and down along his freed-up, knitted-together arm. He said he wouldn't give him a prescription for any painkillers but Johnsey was to go to a chemist and get himself something the name of which he couldn't remember but it was written down on a bit of paper and anyway it was probably going to be a damp squib after the stuff they pumped into him at the hospital because anyone could walk in off the street and buy it without a prescription from a doctor. There was nothing on the telly only your man of the Kyles roaring at English bowsies about using condoms and that big black American lady that makes all the bigshot white women cry. The telly during the day would often depress you more than entertain you.

He thought about Packie Collins with his sour auld puss and wondered how was the little foreign lad getting on below with him. He was still a small bit shocked at how he had been able to tell Packie where to go. That's one thing you can say for having great violence done to you — it gives you a bit of toughness. To hell with Packie Collins and his rolling eyes and angry auld jowls, he could make little of the little foreign lad now instead and see whether *he'd* take it as quietly. That box of papers upstairs would surely realize enough for a man to live in comfort while he thought about things a bit more and tried to see would he sooner stay or go. Anyway, wasn't he a *millionaire on paper* as people kept telling him? What reception would he get in the next life, he wondered, if he entered it landless? Would Granddad and Daddy and the great-uncles and beautiful Uncle Michael be above waiting, wanting to know what sort of a blackguard was he? Would Mother even bother with him? Lord save us and guard us, it's a solid fright knowing nothing, not even how to feel.

★   ★   ★

The ticks and tocks of the old clock were day by day starting to turn back to drips and drops that might for a finish become those Chinese hammer blows bonging through his brain. Was it Monday or Tuesday? What use of names had his days, anyway? You only need put names on days when you have places to go and things to do. *I'll collect you to go hurling training on Tuesday evening so. We'll go for a few pints on Friday night. Will we go in to the cinema on Sunday?* It seemed as though having a break from being lonesome made it ten times worse when you were once again lonesome. Being in the hospital was like the time Daddy was *in remission* from the cancer. That means it went away for a while. But then it came back and killed him.

The house felt quare again. It felt even emptier than it had once Mother's funeral was done and dusted and the last of the biddies had flapped away and the relations felt they had given enough of themselves to warrant at least a couple of indulgences. It was probably the first time in several lifetimes that the house had been completely empty for more than a few days. It was as though the air had congealed, like a bowl of gravy that was left stand undisturbed too long. The Unthanks had tightened up before he arrived, but still there was a staleness about the place. Maybe it had been there before, but he hadn't noticed. Now his nose was used to that sharp hospital smell and his healing eyes were used to clean whiteness. He longed to be back in the hospital. He didn't want to go up the stairs. He felt like he was being watched, and the watchers weren't kindly ancestors but vengeful spirits who had taken occupancy of the empty house and were raging over his return. He slept on the couch with the telly on and the telephone ladies gesturing out at him with their pouty lips and winking eyes. He dreamt of Siobhán and woke with the sound of her in his ears. Outside, the door of the slatted house was still broken and stuck ajar, and the look of the darkness within felt as familiar and safe as a mother's womb must feel to her little unborn baby.

★   ★   ★

A person walked across his view one hot, still day and gave him such a fright his heart nearly leapt from his chest and his arse lost its grip on the hard edge of the old couch and he fell sideways onto the floor. Old Paddy Rourke was abroad in the yard! Johnsey had never before felt such happiness at the sight of a visitor. Normally, his heart would sink at the prospect of small talk. Now he wanted it more than anything. People weren't as inclined to be sympathizing with you over getting bet up as they were over your mother and father dying. Violence embarrassed people. They didn't know the words to use for it. He nearly ran out through the door to meet him.

Paddy wasn't a man for niceties or how's yourself or any news or talk about the weather or the price of milk or beasts. He was looking about the yard and in through the crack in the door of the slatted house. The cloud of shame that Johnsey now understood a bit better seemed to have been lifted from him. Probably he had no regard for Johnsey, anyway, and so would not be ashamed opposite him.

He was as clane and tidy a farmer as you'd ever meet, your father was, God rest him. That was as small as Paddy's talk got. Paddy was stooped and wrinkled and the bit of hair he had left was wispy and white, but you could sense the toughness off of him, it was in his eyes and his voice and the way he clenched and unclenched his fists while he talked. Paddy walked to the wall that ran from the near gable of the slatted house to the front-right edge of the proper house and leaned against it, looking out into the haggard, empty now of all but thistles and briars. He started to speak without turning his eyes from the haggard and the clump of old oak trees beyond it.

Jackie would turn in his grave, lad, if he thought you were going to give the rest of your days letting yourself be blackguarded. He thought the sun rose from behind you and set before you, you know. He made you soft, mind you; he never let you out from behind him. That was one great disservice he done you. You see, he thought his toughness would be poured directly into you. That's not the way it always goes, though. God is heavy-handed with that auld jug for some and then goes easy for others. You can't time him. The finest bull and the fattest heifer often made a wobbly auld meely-mawly of a calf that could hardly stand on its own legs. He had a right to leave you off at times to run and fall and get into scrapes and get the bangs and knocks that hardens young fellas. But he'd let no one look sideways at you. Lookit, there's no sense in that talk, those wrongs can't be righted now. I'm old, Johnsey, and too shook to be going after lads. I'd only make a show of myself, and end up tied to a bed beyond in the county home. They'd take me for an old madman with that *old timers'* disease, you know, where fellas and wans go pure soft and have to be fed their dinner and it all mashed up like a baby's pandy and they don't know their arses from their elbows any more. But you have rakes of time left. Years and years where you can be a man and live happy or you can die a thousand deaths.

Now, every little sneaky prick in the country is watching to see what'll you do about the land. Well, Johnsey, while they're all fixated on the land, and counting money they haven't yet got and might never get, you have a right to take down your father's gun, load both barrels with duck-shot cartridges and bowl down to that pump for yourself and riddle them fuckers that gave you that hiding. Bang, bang. That's the only language they know, boy. Duck shot won't kill nobody, you know. Twill blister the fuckers, though. Twill sting like holy hell. I'll give you it. They'll think the divil himself rose up and whipped the legs off of them. They won't forget it in a hurry, that lesson. Aim low, son, and central. There's woeful spread in duck shot. Two cartridges will pepper the four bollixes. The guards told you there wasn't one thing they could do to them fellas after the hiding they gave you and you nearly dead after it. Well, they can tell the same thing to those boys while the grand nurses beyond inside in the hospital is plugging their holes: Jaysus, sorry for your trouble, lads, but we has no evidence. Not a screed, boys, terrible sorry. Otherwise you'll be forever more regretting you left them away scot-free. Regrets like that never leave you, son. Regrets like that are like *cancer*, the very same as your father got. They eat you from the inside out.

⋆ ⋆ ⋆

Johnsey had nearly forgotten about the guards. It was hard keeping things in line inside your head. The same two as had originally visited full of auld shapes had called back to him again in the hospital the morning after the day of Siobhán's special visit to let him know that that fella with the three initials you'd often hear talked about on the news — the *Dee Pee-Pee* — had sent them back their auld file because it was no good, there was a *lack of evidence* and therefore Eugene Penrose and the townie lad and the other two goonballs would be left away with their crime. The news hadn't bothered Johnsey as much as it had Mumbly Dave, who gave the rest of that day giving out stink about the great injustice that had been perpetrated and the *Dee Pee-Pee* may as well have kicked you in the head himself and what he'd like to do to lads who went four-on-one and they were only scum and them fuckin guards were no use anyway and Johnsey had had to nearly pretend to be more cross about it than he actually was because without the hiding there'd have never been a Lovely Voice or a Mumbly Dave.

He couldn't be saying that to Paddy Rourke, though. He was rightly up in arms. There were two little clouds of white froth at either side of his mouth and when he looked straight at Johnsey his eyes were shining like something was burning behind them. The best thing about Paddy was you hadn't to say much to him, ever. He would pour out his few words, there'd be no milk or sugar added, only a big cup of scalding truth and you could drink it or refuse it, it was all the one to Paddy. Johnsey got the impression that Paddy would sooner he just kept completely silent and reached into the attic for the under-and-over and went down to the pump a-shooting, like Clint Eastwood at the end of *Unforgiven*.

Imagine if he did! There'd surely be no more secret favours from lovely nurses then, that was for certain. Only big old criminals covered in scars and tattoos to share a little cell with above in Mountjoy and doubtless they'd go at him like those fellas went at your man Andy Doo-frane in

The Shawshank Redemption. If it was certain that he was going to fall into the darkness in the slatted house for good, then he could for sure try and put a few holes in them boys, if only for Paddy's sake. It must be easier shoot a man than hit him; you could do it from a distance. Doubtless it would warrant a few more years in Purgatory, but how bad could that be? As far as he knew all you had to do was float about the place feeling sorry for your sins and for throwing the life God gave you back in His face and saying Acts of Contrition and wait to be admitted to paradise. And wasn't it full of little baby angels who had not survived on this earth long enough to be christened? Or was that Limbo? Or were they the same place? Or hadn't the pope released all them little innocent souls into paradise lately? Something like that had happened, he was sure. How's ever, he'd surely never be consigned to hell over a few holes in them bowsies.

Paddy still looked vexed. It looked as though he was going to wait for Johnsey to say something after all. But he didn't. He turned away from the wall and made shapes as if to leave, then he stopped and turned and started talking again.

One other thing, boy, and listen to me now. Once that auld lease is up, don't give it to them again in the name of Jaysus. Them McDermotts is fuckin snakes. They'll take thirteen leases, they've already had four, and they know you'll have notten wrote down about leases nor rent because they knows well you're the same as your father that way — and next thing they'll grab all inside in the courthouse by making out you're soft in the head and they had the use of the land for twelve year under no agreement nor never paid no rent, and the law *abhors* wasted land and twill be given them because of *adverse possession* you see. That's a fancy name they put on squatters' fuckin rights! Tinkers does it wholesale, Johnsey. And you can be sure them McDermotts will do it too. Clear them now and farm your own land or sell it or sell some of it but in the name of Jaysus don't leave it to them rats beyond. How it is them Unthanks haven't all this said to you is beyond me. Poor Sarah hadn't her right mind after Jackie died; I don't blame *her* for leaving things go to pot.

He turned away again and swatted the air once with his hand as he walked as much as to say to hell with this, you're only a gom, I'm wasting precious time trying to talk sense to you. With a hawk and a spit he was through the gap and gone. Johnsey felt like running after him and grabbing his arm and imploring him to stay a while, to at least drink a mug of tea and maybe tell more about the plans for shooting yahoos and clearing McDermotts and maybe he'd explain the secret of filling lonesome days for years on end and Johnsey could in return reveal his secret about Siobhán and surely Paddy Rourke would think more highly of him if he knew he'd had relations with a beautiful nurse and he might take back some of what he said about Johnsey being like a meely-mawly of a calf. But he knew further talk would only make him feel more foolish. Better to accept that men like

Paddy started conversations, had them and ended them with no need of input from the likes of Johnsey Cunliffe, the disgraceful end to a long line of great men. Men like Paddy said their piece and shagged off and wouldn't countenance backchat.

Johnsey longed for Siobhán and Mumbly Dave. He wondered if he fell and split himself open would he land back inside in his grand semi-private room and would she be there to receive him and would Mumbly Dave still be inside, bullshitting out of him and smiling and laughing non-stop and slagging the nurses and being forward and annoying and forcing people against their will to like him? More likely he'd be consigned to the mental ward if he kept up this auld cribbing and moping about the place.

The morning sun was fairly beaming down and all the trees were heavy with green and there was a haze of flies and bugs and butterflies about the land and all he could do was think about how some lives are full to bursting with people and work and sport and children and fun and his own was all empty spaces where those things ought rightly to be, were he the kind of a man that could close his fist around opportunity and keep a tight howlt of it rather than shrinking from it and hiding inside in his parents' house nearly too scared to even peep out for fear of failure and ridicule. Why couldn't he have been born with a full quota of manliness?

★ ★ ★

He waited until Paddy's words settled softly on the cracked ground and the air was again still. There was a coldness around the door of the slatted house, despite the sun's best efforts. The door let out a sigh as he pushed it inwards, as if giving out about his return. He stood in the opening with the sun warming his back and the darkness inside cold on his face. He remembered how he had tried to work out how best to fasten a rope to the crossbeam, how to get himself up to the required height, how to fashion a noose properly, whether it would be best to jump outwards a little off the edge of the enclosure or just drop his whole weight straight down. He remembered thinking first about Mother and then about the Unthanks and even about the aunties and the biddies and how it would upset them in different ways; some would be truly sad and more would be embarrassed, and once or twice he pictured Eugene Penrose and the yahoos and how they'd be smirking about the village as he was waked and letting on to be reverent and full of sorrow as they sniggered with their heads bowed and they crossing themselves as his little cortége passed on its way to the Height and no one who walked behind the hearse would realize he was being mocked even as he was being carried to his place of rest, in between Mother and Daddy in the warm earth.

He backed out into the sun, away from the sharp, cold stink. He resolved there and then that there would be no further considerations of mortal sin in the slatted house. He decided to go upstairs and look in the famous box of papers in

143

Daddy's office. That'd give things to think about besides them old black notions surfacing and whether or not he'd ever clap eyes on Siobhán again let alone feel her lovely soft fingers gripping him and whether he really wanted to go to a pub with Mumbly Dave, it would surely only lead to more embarrassment and situations he would be unable to fit himself into and it was all the one anyway, that fella had no notion of calling up for him no more than the man in the moon.

Dermot McDermott was doing the second cut of silage abroad. Johnsey could hear the big John Deere beyond, roaring over and back across the river field, Daddy's favourite field of all. He wouldn't have cut silage in it and upset the lives of the creatures of the riverbank; he always had the few dull acres down towards the village set aside for silage. No sign of that shagger back looking to buy the land; he knew he was caught out in a lie about milk quotas and what have you. The McDermotts knew all about this rezoning business long before Johnsey and had planned to pull an awful stroke. Let them, to hell. Money is their god, Daddy would have said, and they may as well enjoy it now. It's easier for a camel to go through the eye of a needle than for a rich man to enter the kingdom of heaven. That was one of Daddy's excuses for his lack of cuteness. Them McDermotts would manage it, though. They'd stand above at the Pearly Gates and bamboozle Saint Peter with their wounded faces and assertions of righteousness, the same way they do be cocked up above in Mass directly in Father Cotter's view, looking like the church was built around them. He headed for the front door and the famous box of papers with the whooping cough of the John Deere being rammed into gear in pure crossness grinding against his eardrums.

* * *

That box had nothing in it only confusion. Bits of letters and yokes from banks and insurance companies with big words and lists of figures and two Credit Union books, one with his name in it and one with Mother's and Daddy's names together. God only knows how a fella would go about converting these things into cash-money. He had a card and four numbers Mother had made him remember and he was able to use that at the hole-in-the-wall below in the village to take out money that Packie Collins had put into his account every week, but he had rarely bothered before Mother died and now he only used about thirty or forty quid a week for the few bits to have in the house, like milk and ham and biscuits and them frozen yokes that was easy do in the microwave.

Now that he had given himself the road out of his bit of a job, Packie's money would sooner or later run out. He'd have to make proper shapes at them auld bits of paper then. There was a button you could press that said *balance enquiry* on the hole-in-the-wall. He'd have to see about pressing it one of the days. Feck it to hell, this auld box was too much trouble. He

145

had a right to listen months ago when these things were being explained besides sitting there like a gom and wondering how long would it be before he could stop nodding and saying Oh right, grand.

He walked down as far as his own room for a look out of the window at the yard. It was hard not to look out and harder again not to expect to see Daddy swinging in on his bicycle or Mother chugging through the gate in the Fiesta, barely clearing the piers. One of them teachers inside in the Tech had explained one time what *seeing* really was. He'd thought about it a lot when he was blind. When you look at a thing, the light of the sun bounces off of that thing and into your eye and a message is sent from your *retina* on along up the *optic nerve* to your brain, which then tells you what it is you're seeing by forming a picture for you. So you don't really see a thing as it is, only your brain's version of what it is. Johnsey learnt all that stuff off by heart and wrote it out in an exam one time and still only got a D. D for dunce. He'd memorized the seeing stuff so well he'd left no room for the other bits. What about it, it was all the one now. His detached retina was attached again and it was working away the solid finest and it was now sending light up along that old optic nerve to his bit of a brain which was showing him a picture of a person in rolled-up shirt sleeves and important-looking trousers and a fine, shiny, bald spot coming in along the yard. It was that man of the Grogans who owned the shop and the undertakers and what have you below in the

146

village that used to grig Mother something awful. Oh Lord, what now?

★ ★ ★

He took Johnsey's hand in both of his and started speeching out of him without preamble. Like Paddy Rourke, except while Paddy's speech was about how Johnsey should shoot Eugene Penrose and the yahoos, this speech was about how Johnsey should sell the land, without delay, to a consortium of mainly locals who had progress and employment at their heart. Surely Jackie had told him all about it; it was going on years, this planning for the *land bank*, sure wasn't Jackie as much a driving force behind the whole idea as anyone, sure hadn't he *lobbied* for the rezoning, and now that the planners had seen sense all that was left was for a deal to be done with regard to the sale of the land and plans could be submitted for the *redevelopment* and work could begin almost immediately. Wasn't it a heartbreaking thought that Jackie, Lord have mercy on him, wouldn't see his plans come to fruition? But wouldn't he be happy that the council inside had saw sense at last and his son and his son's children please God could prosper because of him?

This man who had hardly looked in Johnsey's direction below in the village in twenty-four years was now grasping his hand the very same way people did at Mother and Daddy's funerals and was smiling with his lips peeled back from his teeth and gums like a German Shepherd and breathing hot words all over him.

Herbert Grogan said You know I was a great friend to your father, Johnsey. Everyone knows that. I had great regard for him, and he for me. He was no daw, Johnsey. He could see past his own nose, not like some. There's fellas going to sleep poor tonight, Johnsey, that'll wake up tomorrow millionaires. Cattle that was eating ordinary grass yesterday is shitting gold today. This all happens, Johnsey, without any effort on the part of them fellas. They were up early milking and foddering all their lives and doing the same few auld jobs day in, day out, with no thought beyond going to the mart and buying and selling a few beasts and waiting to see what would they be handed in the line of a grant from Europe or what have you. All the effort and fightin and pullin and draggin and Jaysus hardship that makes all them magical millions appear for them fellas is done by the likes of me. Feckin eejits that we are, we can see potential, po-*tential*, Johnsey, in them miserable wet fields where neither beast nor man ever really thrived, for something great that'll benefit all and give jobs and security and happiness. That's all we want to do, Johnsey, is give jobs and better this community and build for the future. Some says we're mad. More says we're *visionaries*. More again calls us crooks and says we're only in it for all we can get for ourselves! Lookit, John, I don't give one shite what any of them says about me, there's as many auld begrudgers around here that wants to see no one have anything only themselves as there always was — the same auld

148

crowd that used sell their neighbours to the English long ago. Let them off to hell, Johnsey, they'll die bitter and there'll be no tears shed for them.

★   ★   ★

Isn't it a fright to God to say a man could end up being a bar to progress and could deny jobs to half the village and wealth to all just by being alive and that the low esteem he was held in by his fellow man could be further reduced by matters in which he had no hand, act nor part? Doesn't that just bate all? Seemingly the whole village was all of a sudden looking out of their mouths at him to know what would he do about selling the land to this *consortium* of bigshots so they may get on with their plans for houses, shops, a school, new roads and what have you. And none of it for profit — all them great men wants is to *give employment*, according to Herbert Grogan. The Creamers and the McDermotts and Paddy Rourke had apparently all already entered into *agreement-in-principle* with regard to their share of this famous land deal. Johnsey wished Paddy had explained more to him about this business instead of telling him he was a meely-mawly and urging him to do impossible violence.

The box in Daddy's office seemed like a pathetic thing now. All of Mother and Daddy's work, the foddering and milking and calving and lambing and shearing and up and down and over and back to mart and abattoir and co-op and all

149

of Mother's saving up and putting away and rows with Daddy over having notions and throwing money around and all of Daddy's long, hard, slogged-out days of laying blocks and they may as well have sat on their arses and drew the dole and watched television all their lives because the few quid that would be the realization of them bits of paper in Daddy's box would be like pebbles inside in a quarry when compared to the sort of money the bigshots wanted to pay for the land.

Johnsey thought again of Our Lord after his forty lonesome days and nights and he famished and parched in the desert and the devil creeping around with offers of thirst quenched and hunger sated and all the riches of the world. And all Jesus wanted to do was tramp the road with his pals and tell all about His Father. It must have been great until them bitter Pharisees told on Him and the Romans got thick. It must have been brilliant having all those friends and magical powers to feed the multitudes and make wine from water and the dead arise and appear to many. What had he? A farm of land already usurped and about to be grabbed away for good and covered over with concrete and no pals to speak of and barely power enough to turn on the washing machine.

That Grogan man was finished talking. Now he was looking at Johnsey with his bottom lip shoving his top lip up towards his pointy nose like one of those men who don't roar and shout at matches, only watch quietly with their arms crossed. Was he waiting for Johnsey to say something? At least he wouldn't say *I'll have to ask* this time. Should he invite him in? A vampire has to be invited in; otherwise they can't cross your threshold.

Johnsey told Herbert Grogan he was going to talk to his accountant and thanked him for calling up and backed up the yard towards the front door with one hand reaching behind to guide him in. Once he had the door closed he stood still a while and waited for the sound of retreating footsteps and an engine starting outside the gate and when these sounds came he could breathe again and wonder where he came up with *I'm going to talk to my accountant!*

Good man, Johnsey, begod. It sure was better than *I'll have to ask!*

August

There's a poem a fella wrote about how he'd see old men who reminded him of how his father looked when he died. He said

> *Every old man I see*
> *Reminds me of my father*
> *When he had fallen in love with death*
> *One time when sheaves were gathered.*

Johnsey learnt that whole poem off by heart in school. Now he only remembered that first verse. August is the very start of autumn. Some things ripen in August, having drunk the sunshine all summer. Other things start to die and fall away to nothing. You'd always start to feel the nip in the air in August. You'd be scalded red at a match and by the time you arrived home that evening the sun would have tired from the fight and would have let the cold, white moon chase it back behind the hills. The sun does be weaker in August, watery, not able to keep a whole day warm.

Daddy died in August. All that last summer, while all about him grew and bloomed, Daddy shrank and slowly died. He fell in love with death, like your man's father.

* * *

152

Mumbly Dave arrived on the first day of August, and everything changed. Johnsey spotted him coming from the haggard wall. He came in the gate nearly sideways, revving like a madman and his tyres screeching their protest at his showing off, in one of them cars that used to make Daddy shout Look at that feckin YAHOO when they went flying up the road past the gate. Johnsey's heart cartwheeled in his chest. Imagine feeling such joy at the sight of a fat little *plámáser*! Mumbly Dave hugged Johnsey, like one of them Mafia lads. It felt like falling into a pile of hay that was warmed by the sun after a long day's labour. He drew back fast for fear Mumbly Dave would sense his enjoyment and think he was a queer. Mumbly Dave was talking away ninety. No change there. He had a fine mouth of permanent falsies, so gone was the Mumbly and all that was left was Dave. He spun full circle for fear he wouldn't see something and next thing he was gone, darting through the gap between the slatted house and the workshop into the big yard on his short legs before Johnsey could protest.

Johnsey didn't like the big yard; it was too full of nothing now where once it was a place of running muck and beasts passing on their way to the parlour and Daddy's *hups* and *shcoo-ons* and the smell of shit and diesel fumes. But now that Mumbly Dave had planted himself in the middle of it, it seemed more alive again, less like one of them ghost towns you'd see on a Western and more like a place that could be woken out of its sleep and put to use again.

Mumbly Dave read Johnsey over leaving Daddy's Land Rover and Mother's Fiesta to crumble and rot, and promised to get them going. He marvelled at the size of the hay barn and guessed you could ram twenty apartments into it. *Ha?* Course you could. No Jaysus bother, boy. He darted in and out of the outhouses, jabbering away all the time, for all the world like one of them chubby monkeys that swing around the trees below in Fota Island.

By Jaysus, youssir, I'll tell you one thing, you're the talk of the village below. There's some maintains you're after *twenty million* for this place! You're dead fuckin right, youssir. *Twenty . . . Jaysus . . . million.* Dave paused to shake his head and whistle. And you know what? You're dead fuckin right! Woo-hoo, boy! Them fuckin McDermotts and the Collinses and their big leader Herbie Grogan and the rest of the con-fuckin-*sortium* as they call themselves, you have 'em quare fuckin *rattled*, boy!

It didn't seem fair to knock the wind out of his sails. Just by doing nothing, too afraid nearly to venture past the gate, save for first Mass on Sundays, he had the village below in uproar. Signs on he'd been getting quare looks above at the church and along the road home. He'd thought it was to do with the beating but now it seemed it was more to do with him being a money-hungry blackguard and trying to fleece all them hard-working business men and they only trying to give jobs to people and make the world a better place. He seemed to have made Mumbly Dave happy at least. He thought of

154

Paddy Rourke and his wife the time of the wild calf and how Paddy was condemned as a man who'd beat up a woman. Mother was right. People will think and say and believe what pleases them. The truth is what's shouted loudest and by the most. What about it? Let them all off to hell. That's what Daddy would have said.

Johnsey told Mumbly Dave all about Herbert Grogan and his big auld spiel and how he'd told lies about Daddy having planned all along to sell the land and how it was Daddy tried to get the land rezoned originally and all about Dermot McDermott trying to trick him into selling the land to them because they were *mar dhea* after getting a bigger milk quota and wanted to be *sure of the land*, and Mumbly Dave shook his head and spat like Paddy Rourke and said how them Grogans would buy you and sell you and they'd tell you black was white and that McDermott was only a bollix anyway, and his people were pure grabbers, sure the whole place knew that.

Mumbly Dave wanted to know how's it they was never friends years ago? Johnsey ventured that they went to separate schools and were a good few years apart, anyway. Mumbly Dave allowed that this was so, and said he was forever forgetting that Johnsey was only twenty-*four*. Johnsey never heard talk of friendship before between two men. He wondered had Daddy and Jimmy Unthank and Paddy Rourke ever declared themselves to be friends, or was their bond left go unmentioned, unmolested by words? Johnsey

155

got the impression that Mumbly Dave could talk himself into things and out of things until the cows came home and none of his declarations of friendship or enmity would carry much weight when all was said and done. But still and all, for days like this, when that auld clock inside was ticking and tocking its cruel beat and a man had little to do besides look in over the haggard wall and wonder how a universe so packed with stuff could have left a space this empty, Mumbly Dave's declarations of fondness and friendship, weighty or not, were as welcome as the sun when there was hay waiting to be saved or turf to be footed.

★ ★ ★

For a finish, Mumbly Dave called up nearly every day that August. The days he didn't call stretched out their legs and took their own sweet, maddening time in passing. Those days, he looked at the telly and the telly looked back and outside the milky sun shone down on a world that seemed to be going to waste when there was no Mumbly Dave to go out into it with. The days he did call galloped past, because that's the way time is — it's not a *constant* either, like that science teacher said. Going to town in Mumbly Dave's car to look at wans in miniskirts or walking down the Callows and firing stones into the river like bold children or sitting around the kitchen looking out at the rain and drinking a few cans of Harp with Mumbly Dave talking and talking and talking all the time — doing these things made time speed up so you'd barely be finished laughing at Mumbly Dave's slagging of a wan's fat arse or some fella's gimpy walk or a young fella with the head dyed off of himself or whatever new tall tale he had to tell and you'd look at your watch and you'd realize you were going to miss *Home and Away* and you didn't even care.

Mumbly Dave was going to claim a fine whack of money off of Timmy Shaughnessy who everyone called Timmy Shake Hands on account of how he'd always greet you with a handshake. Timmy owned the stand on which he'd placed his ladder, which had then collapsed and spilled ladder and Dave onto the hard ground and his fall only broken by the edge of a wall and the ladder was the finest but you know yourself how *I* fared out, wasn't I in smithereens? And Timmy Shake Hands could claim recompense from the council who owned the house the gutters of which he was cleaning and sure they could claim from the Board of Works who had ordered that the house be tidied up in the first place and the house should have been knocked long ago anyway and wasn't that what insurance was for, to compensate a man for his pain and suffering? And that solicitor lady was taking no prisoners, that was for sure. She was a fine thing too, bejaysus.

Mumbly Dave had the world of stories about things he'd done and seen and places he'd been and women he'd gotten off with. He'd shifted every girl who was roughly his age in the parish and most of the girls in surrounding parishes. He

157

was solid *red* from riding. He'd even point at wans inside in *town* and claim to have gotten a shag off of them! Besides making himself out to be a great lover of women, Mumbly Dave was forever telling stories about *the lads*. Me and the lads, one time, we went away to Cork for the weekend. Jaysus youssir, twas some craic. Me and one of the lads took two cracking women home one time and one a them turned out to be an awful lunatic and she went for your man with a broken wine glass, twas a solid scream! Me and the lads used be forever fighting with them townies inside in the nightclub and one night I was cornered by three of the bowsie fuckers and I was on my own on account the lads had all gone away early but I nutted one prick in the snout and lamped another in the balls full force and the third bollix turned and ran and I didn't even bother chasing him, only stopped a cab, and there was a wan waiting for a cab as well and we said Feck it to hell, we'll share, and I ended up shifting the face off of her in the back of the cab and as I was paying your man he just looked at me and shook his head and he just said *Legend*.

Johnsey never saw any of these lads, though, nor heard their names. When Mumbly Dave blew his horn and saluted fellas along the road with the back of his hand flat against his windscreen, they as a rule returned his friendliness with a bare raised finger or nod of the head or not at all. And Mumbly Dave never made good on his promise to bring Johnsey for a few pints. Sure what harm? A few tall tales never

hurt anyone, and he had survived grand so far
without going to pubs. Mother often said
someone she enjoyed was a *tonic*. Like that
person was good for her. Now he knew what she
meant.

★   ★   ★

The phone hopped most days, and when he
answered it people wanted to ask him questions
and tell him things and talk about auctions and
commission and what he wanted to do and for a
finish he found a volume yoke on the bottom of
the phone and he turned it down to the last and
that was an end to the torture of having to
mumble half-truths to strangers and hang the
phone up on them. But that was only like when
that little Dutch fella stuck his finger in the hole
in the dam — he could feel the pressure building
up in the silent phone of all the unanswered calls
and all the people wanting to talk to him and ask
him things and tell him how much he could
make and what an opportunity he'd been
handed and after a few days he could hardly
walk past the hall table where the phone sat
without feeling like it was going to go BANG
and burst all over him and drown him in angry
voices and big urgent words.

After a few visits, Mumbly Dave took to
walking straight in, without knocking on door or
window. The first time he did it, he stood in the
doorway of the kitchen looking in at Johnsey and
Johnsey looked back at him from the table where
he was eating a cut of toast and having a sup of

tea and Mumbly Dave asked him had he a problem *mar dhea* he was going to fight with Johnsey and Johnsey tried to stop himself laughing and told him he had some neck sauntering in like he owned the place and Mumbly Dave said he was very sorry, it was just that Sir Godfrey Blueballs the Butler seemed to be indisposed today, otherwise he'd have announced his arrival, you bollix, and they both started laughing and sure what about it if he walked straight in, you'd hear him coming from the far end of the village in his yahoo car, anyway.

That's how Johnsey got caught with the newspaper fella. It was getting on towards half-eleven one day, the time Mumbly Dave normally arrived and they'd drink a mug of tea and eat a Mikado or a cut of tart if the Unthanks had been up before, planning whether they'd have a city day, a video day, a cans-of-Harp day or a do-nothing day. The doorbell rang and Johnsey roared Come in, it's open, and just as he was wondering why the Jaysus Mumbly Dave had reverted to doorbell-ringing, a right-looking quare-hawk presented himself at the kitchen door and smirked and said Mister Cunliffe I presume, like that fella that went looking for the other fella in the jungle, in one of those accents like you hear now and again if you've the car window down and it's lunchtime in the city and there's young lads passing the car from the posh school, Mount Something. The quare-hawk said he worked for a newspaper and he had a square yoke with his picture on it and small writing and

160

he wanted to know could he ask Johnsey a few questions about his part in the local land deal and Johnsey felt that tightness in his stomach and lightness in his balls that he'd hoped he'd never feel again, and he wasn't even sure why. He said No, you can't, I thought you were someone else, that's why I said to come in, you'll have to go, and the posh-accent lad said Oh right, no problem, so I'll just put *no comment* will I, because everyone else around here has a comment about *you*, and the way he said *you* it sounded like he couldn't stand Johnsey and thought he was better than him. He had the head of a right dipstick, Daddy would have said.

The quare-hawk was backing along the hall and Johnsey was walking towards him and he kept talking all the time, asking was it true that Johnsey wanted twenty million for the land and was he aware that the planning authority had given provisional approval to plans by a local development company that were contingent on the sale and did he feel he could just name his price because of this and did he have any feelings of guilt? And just as he backed through the door and into the yard, another lad, with a spotty, sneaky face, walked out from behind the jeep that must have free-wheeled into the yard because Johnsey hadn't heard it coming, and he took Johnsey's photo with a camera that looked more like a machine gun. And then they were in the jeep, and the posh lad stuck his arm out and there was a little card on the end of it and Johnsey took it off him and the posh lad said If you change your mind about making a

161

comment, give me a *coal*, and they were gone. Give him a coal? Oh, ya, a *call*.

Minutes later when Mumbly Dave arrived, Johnsey was still in the yard and he took a while explaining to Mumbly Dave what had happened because he was shaking a small bit even though it was fine and warm and he felt like crying but he wasn't sure why and Mumbly Dave told him not to worry about them pricks to hell and slapped his hand against Johnsey's back as they walked up the yard, and isn't it great to have a pal to put his hand on your back and tell you not to worry?

* * *

The next Sunday, before Johnsey had even got out of bed to get dressed for Mass, he heard Mumbly Dave's trumpet exhaust blowing down the Dark Road towards the house. He burst in the front door past Johnsey and landed in to the kitchen with his face shining red, waving a newspaper. Johnsey felt a burning in his stomach as Mumbly Dave placed the paper on the kitchen table like a priest laying the chalice with the host on the altar and Mumbly Dave was opening the pages slowly and shaking his head and saying *Youssir* . . . wait . . . till . . . you . . . fucking . . . see . . . *this*!

There were three huge black words across the top of the page: LAND OF GREED. Below that there were loads more words, smaller than those, but still bigger than the normal-sized words that filled the rest of the two pages:

This is the young bachelor from rural Tipperary whose obscene demands are threatening to derail plans to transform the fortunes of an entire community.

And beside that writing was a fuzzy picture of a fella with two red cheeks and his mouth half open and one eye half closed and a cross look on his puss and feck it all to hell, it was *himself*. He looked at Mumbly Dave, and the prick was so excited he was nearly mounting the kitchen table. Aboy Johnsey, aboy Johnsey, you fuckin legend, he kept saying over and over again.

The rest of the words told about how

this young bachelor, who has turned a deaf ear to his neighbours' appeals for sanity in his approach to the brokering of a massive property deal, was left the land by his late parents and has shown little interest in working the land, choosing instead to lease the farm to neighbours and live a life of luxury in the period farmhouse that his late parents spent tens of thousands of pounds renovating. Since being assaulted by a group of unemployed locals, angry at his cavalier attitude to their futures, he has become a virtual recluse, issuing his crazed demands through a firm of city accountants. One local, who asked not to be named, had this to say: 'No one would condone what happened [to Cunliffe] but you can see why the likes of them lads would be angry. He's above sitting pretty, he can't lose, and he could give the rest of his life living in the lap of luxury either way. No one hereabouts knows where this greedy streak comes from. His father and mother was the salt of the earth, God rest them. God alone knows how someone from such good, decent stock could turn out that way.'

Then, at the bottom, it said *See Analysis, page 34*. It was hard to find page 34 with shaky, sweaty hands. Page 34 had a picture of a curly-haired fella with roundy glasses and fat cheeks and a right scowl on his puss and his arms folded as much as to say nothing gets past me, boy, I'll sort ye all out. Johnsey didn't like the look of him one bit. And the fat-cheeked curly lad wasn't too impressed with Johnsey either. Below his picture, he had written a fine big spiel. Mumbly Dave took the paper off of Johnsey and cleared his throat *mar dhea* he was a right important lad about to make a speech. Then he read out the curly fella's words in a posh accent and sure, listening to him, you wouldn't know whether to laugh or cry.

Mumbly Dave read:

Many things have happened to our little Republic in recent times that we'd scarcely have believed possible just a few short years ago. We have become the world's biggest producer of impotency medicine, of all things. Our products are in demand the world over. We have become a hub of global finance. We have become a renowned centre of technology and innovation. We have seen a meteoric rise in the level of degrees, masters and doctoral graduates from our colleges and universities. We have become a net contributor to the European Union. Inward migration has far outstripped emigration. We have next to no unemployment. The only ones lingering on benefits are the terminally lazy, the old and the ill.

These are all good, good things.

But many things have happened that dim this glowing light of dynamism and prosperity and threaten to extinguish it completely.

Our cabinet pays itself more than any other government in the western world. Our public service is growing day by day into a vast, uncontrollable beast, accountable to nobody but its own self-interested self. Home ownership is fast becoming an unattainable dream for many of our young people. The exchequer boasts a surplus of billions, yet just three days ago a man finished his life in a manner devoid of dignity on a trolley in the A and E Department of an Irish hospital because there was no bed for him to lie in and not enough staff to look after him properly.

And now we learn that one of our fellow citizens, a native of a quiet, unremarkable rural parish just like any other, a man who has no reason to think himself special or beyond the exigencies of common decency, has informed his neighbours, the people among whom he has lived for his twenty-four years, that if they are to improve their lives and house their children and secure the future of their little hinterland, they must first pay him this incredible figure: TWENTY MILLION.

Take a moment to digest that figure, my friends. And ask yourself this: If an ordinary, ostensibly decent Irish man is capable of such gross indecency, of such staggering greed, of such arrogance, ask yourselves, fellow Irish men and women, what next? What will we learn next about ourselves and what we're capable of?

Dear God, what next?

That cross newspaper fella had an awful set on him, it seemed. And he was even calling on God to back him up, as much as to say Johnsey was in league with the devil or something. He wasn't full sure what *arrogance* was, or *ostensibly*, and nor was Mumbly Dave, but he didn't think it was anything complimentary. Words were always going to be his enemies, it seemed. You could make anything sound true. A thing that's written down in black-and-white printed words on paper always looks true. He nearly believed *himself* to be a rotten yoke at this stage. Why would anyone doubt them little black words? Wasn't the Bible full of the same little black words, and there was plenty would die before doubting their trueness? You couldn't go around doubting the word of God, but God didn't write it down, for He was above words.

You wouldn't catch God putting his photo above a big old newspaper article to convince people of who was good and who was bad. Even so, a lie in print looks truer than the truth sounds from the mouth of a fool. His best bet was to do nothing, Mumbly Dave advised. Johnsey agreed. He could see how any words he might be able to stutter out in his own defence would only lead to more words in reprisal from them that has far more beautiful control of words and can make them do their will.

Mumbly Dave was gone from his high to being vexed and upset. We is *pals*, Johnsey, d'you know what I mean? There's no few auld fields nor no fat fucker's opinion above in Dublin who doesn't know fuck all about notten goin to change that. We was through the mill together, boy. You made me welcome in your home. We know each other. I'll tell you wan thing, boy, they can all go way and *shite* for themselves. Hey youssir, why should you give wan sugar what that crowd says or does?

Mumbly Dave had tears in his eyes. Then he came around and started to make jokes about the whole thing and Johnsey's shaky feeling started to go away.

★ ★ ★

The truth was a quare thing, anyway, that was plain to see. It could shift beneath you like a hillock that looked firm but was really just grass on wet muck. There was a fella on *The Late Late Show* one time who looked like the devil with his auld eyebrows pointing up at the edges towards heaven as if to mock it and he maintained there was no God and that was the truth. He was an *eighty-ist*. They are people that don't believe in belief. Mother had gone mad and said wasn't it a fright they'd give over people's licence-fee money to put that fella on the television but Daddy only shook his head and said Yerra, Sally, the devil will forever be trying that auld trick.

The trick Daddy meant was to convince people there was only this earthly world and no other, that we all came about by chance and would one day be dust and no more. That way the devil would rule the world: by tricking man into thinking *he* could rule the world and there would be neither judgment nor eternal damnation. Man would sully his soul, believing his soul not to exist. God had a plan for each and every one of us, Daddy declared, and the likes of that long-faced Englishman on the telly had given themselves over to the service of the devil. *That* was the truth.

What if Daddy's truth and the long-faced Englishman's truth met each other halfway, Johnsey wondered? What if there *was* a God, not one who bothered to make plans for people, but who had washed His hands of Man after He fashioned him in His own likeness? The Englishman's story seemed unlikely; there *had* to be a God. Who would have made everything otherwise? But it seemed just as unlikely that this God who was the creator of all things, every winking star and grain of sand and blade of grass, was still going about attending to each person and listening to every stupid thought they had. You had to just believe and think no more about it. But the thing was, that crafty-looking Englishman put them words together so nice, he'd nearly have you doubting Our Lord. Imagine that! The likes of Johnsey, who could barely get a sentence out without his face going on fire and his brain downing tools in protest hadn't much hope against people whose talent lay in arranging words in an order that made them into a solid wall that could never be scaled by contradiction.

What's a lie, anyway? Do you have to know a thing to be not true, or just not care whether or not it's true for the saying of it to be a lie, or are you telling lies if what you say is not true but you think it is? If that quare-looking curly lad in that paper really *believes* Johnsey to be an awful yoke that's destroying the country, does that absolve him of the sin of lying? What would he say, Johnsey wondered, if he came to the house and gave a day gouging around with him and Mumbly Dave? Jaysus lads, I was wrong, sure he's only a gom! He doesn't know his arse from his elbow! The poor boy has his bit to eat and watches the telly and hangs around with a little fat fella and that's all there is to the story. He's one of these people that things happen *to*, not one of them that makes things *happen*. Sorry about that, my mistake. All he is is a victim of circumstance!

★ ★ ★

Famous is a nice word. It glides out of your mouth. Like *Siobhán*. It's a word for those that are known to all, like county hurlers and rock singers and big actors. You can be famous for a lot of different things. You can't be famous for something bad, though. You can be known to all for that bad thing, but there's a different word for that kind of fame. You wouldn't call a fella a *famous* murderer or a *famous* rapist or what have you. Them fellas are called *notorious*. They haven't fame; they have *notoriety*. That word doesn't glide from your mouth. It bangs against your teeth and your tongue tries to tame it and still it sounds ugly, like the noise a creeping lizard might make, or a poison spider. Johnsey was *notorious* for his greed. And he nearly afraid to eat two Mars bars in a row for fear of committing the deadly sin of gluttony.

A lad whose face looked kind of familiar called up in one of them cars that women drive that look like bubbles with googly eyes and wanted to know would Johnsey give his side of the story, and he could be sure of fairness from his own local paper, and there'd be no opinion or twist put into it. Johnsey said he had neither side nor story, but your man wanted to know how was it he was attacked, what did he think his attackers' *motives* were and Johnsey said how the feck would he know and Mumbly Dave came out from the kitchen and ran your man and when he was gone he told Johnsey that fella had always been a little faggotyarse, and he forever camped inside in the courthouse waiting to see how many of his neighbours' names he can destroy in that auld paper. Johnsey was as well off saying notten to them rats.

★ ★ ★

For the first time since he was a small boy panned out with a burning sickness, Johnsey didn't go to Mass by choice that Sunday. Now even God would fall out with him. What about it? The last thing Father Cotter would want, anyway, would be him swaggering up the churchyard, with his *notoriety* in tow, stealing Our Lord's thunder, with the whole place gawking out of their mouths at him and small children checking his arse for a pointy tail.

The Unthanks didn't say anything about the newspaper. That was the thing with the Unthanks: you could sit in their house for hours and barely two sentences might be said but it wouldn't matter a damn. You didn't have to feel any awkwardness at your lack of words in their presence. But just as he was making shapes to leave, Himself said Aren't you as well off get out of that land to hell? And the sudden way he said it and the hint of temper in his voice shocked Johnsey and his brain was trying to grab at words and form them into a queue so that they'd come out his mouth in a proper order when Herself said It'll only cause you trouble now forevermore. It'll break your heart.

Johnsey had had a half an idea that the Unthanks would think it noble and brave of him to not sell the land on account of how Daddy gave his life to it, how he sweated over it and

171

bled into it and killed himself trying to mind it and drag a living out of it, and his father before him did the same, and his father's father. It was like Himself read his mind. He said Yerra, your heart'll be scalded, Johnsey, with blackguards blackening you up and down the country and making up lies about you and it's an awful shame something so good has to be taken over by them that only has their own gain in mind, but that's the way the world is now — you have to leave businessmen off to build these things and let them make their fortunes to hell, and in the long run their greed benefits all.

Johnsey asked why people thought he was after being offered twenty million for the land and Himself said Sure that's only an auld makey-up number, *we* never . . . And Herself made a funny, squeaky noise and belted him into the arm and Himself reddened and closed his eyes and covered his face with his hand, that lovely gentle hand that held Johnsey's tight when there was a crush coming out of Croke Park one time when he was a small boy and he was lifted off of his feet by the crowd and had lost sight of Daddy, and now that lovely hand was shaking and so was the head behind it and Herself looked like she was going to cry, and even a gom like Johnsey could figure out what was after happening: the Unthanks were part of this famous *consortium* and they hadn't wanted him to know, and Himself was after accidentally telling him. And all he wanted to do was tell Himself it was okay, he didn't mind, he loved him anyway, sure what about it, wasn't he as well

172

off to have friends in the enemy's camp? But all he could do was mumble his thanks for the dinner and turn and walk out through the door onto the empty street. And did he *really* hear Herself telling Himself in a shouty whisper he was a *feckin eejit* behind him? Sure, at this stage, anything was possible.

September

Isn't it a fright to God to say that the sun splits the stones at the start of September every single year? The poor little children do be pasty-faced for the want of a sunny day and the very minute they're back at school, it comes out to mock them! How is it at all? And then the crathurs has to go in to school wall-falling with the tiredness after their big trip to Dublin for the All-Ireland. When Tipp is in the final, win or lose, the next day should be a free day, and that's all there is to it. That's the kind of talk you'd always hear at the beginning of September. The sun that was weakening in August, though, was as a rule nearly spent by September. It wouldn't really split the rocks at all; it would hardly even make them lukewarm. But people love giving out, Mother always said.

In September the cooking apples abroad on the trees beside the haggard would be bursting with ripeness and only barely clinging to the branch. Some would have turned to rot on the tree; more would have fallen to the earth — the barest puff of a breeze would dislodge a big fat cooking apple in September. You had to be quick to get to the windfalls before the scavenging insects. You'd pick one up thinking it to be good and turn it to see the other side was brown mush moving with worms and you'd fling it from you in disgust. You had to twist each apple off gently;

174

otherwise no bud would reappear on that spot the next year. Only thick ignoramuses *yanks* apples off of trees, Mother always said. Like Uncle Frank — you couldn't let that fella out to fill a bag for Theresa or you'd have nare a cooking apple of your own to bake a tart ever again. He'd wreck before him, that fella. He didn't fit with nature.

September had its miserable strictness of school's restart and freedom's loss, its watery, mocking sun, and its big anti-climaxes above in Croke Park, but it also had tarts and crumble made with the finest of Mother's own apples that were still ripening an hour before, and that nearly made up for everything.

* * *

Johnsey would fill four or five boxes with apples for the bakery every year. He wondered whether it was best just to leave it this year, or to fill them as normal and have them ready, or to put a box up on his carrier and cycle down to the Unthanks and drop them in and sit down in the kitchen and drink a cup of tea and watch Herself cooking and listen to Mary with the Cod Eye getting *mar dhea* chatted up by them black-guards from the building site out the Ashdown Road and not mention anything to do with land or zones or newspapers or other people's plans or consortiums or what have you. Wouldn't that be the right job?

It was all the one for a finish: the Unthanks arrived in their old Nissan Bluebird on the

Tuesday after the terrible Sunday and Johnsey said nothing about the land thing and nor did they and the three of them crossed the haggard and gathered windfalls in near silence. But now the comfort was gone from that silence and embarrassment had taken its place and they loaded the full bags into the Bluebird's big boot and Himself praised the quality of the apples and promised to prune the trees back and Johnsey said twas grand, *he'd* do it and Himself said no, he loved doing it, wasn't it a fine excuse to be out from under Herself's feet? And he winked at Johnsey in mock conspiracy and Johnsey laughed and Herself asked what were they laughing at as she took Pyrex dishes of dinners out of the Bluebird and took them in to the fridge and everything was lovely and normal and comfortable and destroyed forever at the same time.

★   ★   ★

After the Unthanks had gone away and left Johnsey looking out the window after them with one of those painful lumps in his throat that are surely a blockage caused by a buildup of the words you should have spoken, a red car drove slowly past the gate. There was a blonde girl driving it. He heard the car pull up in the gravel out by the road, and a door slam. The blonde girl walked back past the gate. And a few seconds later, she passed up again in the opposite direction. She slowed and half turned to face into the yard and squinted against the sun and leaned a bit forward as though she needed to get

176

closer to get a better look but didn't dare pass in until she was sure of her place and Johnsey squinted back at her through the cat-scratched kitchen window and Mother of Divine God, it was Siobhán.

Maybe it's better that a man is given no notice of the arrival of a beautiful woman. That way he can't be expected to have readied himself and can be more easily forgiven for looking and sounding like a fool opposite her. Either way, Johnsey knew, he would make an awful bags of it. He couldn't hide behind eye bandages or incapacity now. He'd have to be a proper person. Please God let Mumbly Dave arrive. She was in through the gateway now, starting to pick her steps through the caked yard, waving in at him with one hand and reaching for an invisible handrail with the other to steady her passage. He could see that she was only a couple of steps away from Daddy's boot-worn track — she'd surely stumble and fall. That thought poked him in the back and propelled him out along the hall, his heart kicking at his ribcage. Just as he came through the front door into the yard, the edge of the rut grabbed the sole of her shoe and she was nearly toppled. But she righted herself with two quick steps forward and said Jesus, is this place booby-trapped?

What can you say to something like that? No? Yes? Ha ha? Mumbly Dave would have a funny reply out inside of a second; he'd be over to her like a hot snot, taking her hand to help her across the uneven ground, smart words spilling from his lips. The best Johnsey could do was:

What are you doing here? And he'd hear himself saying those stupid words over and over again for hour after terrible, tortured hour that night. Siobhán said Oh, well that's fucking lovely! After I risk my life to find you in this . . . *bog*! And he tried to take it back: Oh cripes no, I didn't mean that, it's great to see you, I just wasn't expecting . . . And she said Well, I *did* ask my social secretary to liase with yours, but that girl is just *useless* these days. And he looked at her like a gom and said Ha? Name of God, what was she on about? Oh, she was joking. Oh right, he said. Ha ha ha!

He could hear himself: the thickness of his voice, the fakeness of his stupid laugh. It was like the time Mother had made him go on the phone to her brother in Australia on account of he was dying and he was to ask him how was he and tell him he'd say a prayer for him but he knew that Mother's brother was just as embarrassed as he was and he'd have preferred not to have to make small talk with imbecile nephews he'd never seen in the flesh and now never would on account of his kidneys were doing for him and Johnsey burned with mortification and misery and he could hear everything he was saying echoed back along the line from Australia a second after he said it and he could clearly hear how foolish he sounded and his uncle was dead a week later and Mother didn't cry at all nor hardly seemed bothered but then she dropped a small box of eggs that she was only after collecting in the haggard one morning three weeks later and she started

178

crying and didn't stop for the rest of that day.

His brain was pulling against him big time. It was giving him no digout with all this talking, but it'd have a great time for itself later, playing it all back to him, tormenting him, making him want to saw his own tongue off with Mother's old carving knife. It was leaving him down badly, as usual. Making him think of ancient phone calls to Australia and dropped eggs and tearful mothers and what have you in the middle of this emergency situation. What in the name of all that's good and holy was he going to do? Oh God, why send an angel to a fool? What a waste.

She stood and looked at him and he stood looking back at her and he could feel the burning redness igniting around his neck and creeping up along his jaw and she was wearing one of those dresses some women wear in the summer that look as though they'd feel silky to the touch and the sun was playing with her hair and if the world halted itself there and then and the sky exploded and rained down fire he wouldn't have been able to look away. Siobhán asked was he going to invite her in or would she have to stand there in a puddle of cowshit all day? Mumbly Dave would have said something like You could eat your dinner off of that yard, girl, the only cow that does be trotting along here now is Bridie McDermott bringing Johnsey the rent! But Johnsey had no such talent for smartness and he just told her to come in, come in.

★ ★ ★

179

Siobhán told him it wasn't every patient got home visits. As a matter of fact, he was the first patient she'd ever visited at home. She walked from the hall to the good room and looked at everything and then she crossed the hall to the kitchen and she examined the table and the couch and said Jesus, do you have a *cleaner* or something? Or did you get *married* since I saw you last? And all he could do was stand in the hall looking at her like a gom and he just about caught himself in time before he started scratching himself.

No, no, I do be tipping away myself at it, like, while I'm waiting for D . . . How do you explain that you only clean your own house because it makes the time go faster while you wait for the sound of Mumbly Dave's exhaust pipe? There's a word for that manner of carry on: *pathetic*. The last thing you want to do in front of a woman is look pathetic. Only having one friend is pathetic. Only having any sort of a life because of that one friend bothering with you and being constantly frightened he'll get bored and drop you is worse again. It could even be worse than having none; at least then you could make out to yourself that you're too tough to need anyone, you plough a lonely furrow, you're a lone wolf, like John Rambo or your man in *Mission: Impossible*.

Waiting for *who*? Have you a girlfriend? You haven't, I know. I kept track of you, my little blind farmer boy! Sure I had to keep tabs on you. That wasn't a great picture of you in the paper. You wouldn't want to be relying on that

180

now for attracting women. You'd nearly be as well off chancing your arm in Lisdoonvarna than plastering your face all over the newspapers. Johnsey told her how that newspaper fella with the camera had snuck up on him and she said he must have. Anyway, who do you be waiting for? Dave, he told her. What? *Mumbly* Dave?

Her eyes widened and one side of her top lip twisted upwards. Was this the way women talked to men all the time? As though they were trying to catch you out or make a fool of you? Was this flirting, he wondered? It was certainly embarrassing enough. When she used tease him inside in the hospital it was funny; he knew she was only pulling his leg. Now it seemed like she was nearly insulted that he and Dave were friends and the jokiness in her voice and her *mar dhea* surprise sounded like it was half sourness. The shock of her arrival, her scrutiny of the house, her high-pitched questions, the scalding loveliness of her — there were too many things attacking his brain at once. He thought of a cartoon where a lad's head would burst like a balloon. He felt sweat pricking through the skin of his forehead. His brain could marshal not a word to send to his mouth. Oh Lord, he was coming undone. If she went at his mickey now, he'd probably pass out. But then he heard a distant trumpet that rose and fell with the changing of gears — Mumbly Dave was on his way, to save him from himself! And to save Siobhán's lovely eyes from the sight of his exploded brains dripping down the kitchen wall. Thank God for Mumbly Dave.

If you put two boy rats in a cage together, they'll more than likely get on the solid finest, provided they're given a bit to eat and aren't driven mad with the hunger. Put in a girl rat with them, though, and no matter how much food they're given, they'll tear strips off of each other over her and one will kill the other for a finish. That's something Daddy used tell Johnsey to let him know how women could cause terrible trouble for men. Mother used tell him shut up out of it and stop poisoning the boy against women and signs on he used a story about rats to illustrate his point — sure weren't all men the same as rats, really, with their little beady eyes and their little pointy snouts twitching the minute they see a flash of skirt? Then Daddy would smile and tell Johnsey about Helen of Troy and Kitty O'Shea and Maud Gonne and the trouble they caused for men and the downfalls from greatness they brought about, but he'd be all the time casting an eye over to Mother and she'd be ironing or baking and smiling away and shaking her head and Johnsey would know then that Daddy was only trying to get a rise out of her and he didn't really believe all that stuff about how women were awful troublemakers. Still though, he couldn't help remembering Daddy's story about the two boy rats and the girl rat as he listened to Mumbly Dave and the same auld smart talk out of him opposite Siobhán as he used be going on with in the hospital.

The Lovely Voice, in his house. Imagine! And

Mumbly Dave, spouting smartness and doing his best to show off, and she laughing at his auld spiel; it was an almost unbearable pleasure. But now he couldn't sit there dumbly and listen and feel the mad mixture of laughter and jealousy bubbling in his stomach like he had in the hospital; he had no blindness or sickness or weakness to hide behind, he'd have to try and be a proper person who throws out whole lines of conversation, all casual and cool and without making people lean closer and look embarrassed and ask him to repeat himself. He might as well try and sprout a pair of wings and fly about the yard.

Mumbly Dave was telling Siobhán all about Johnsey being a *property tycoon* and how he was sticking to his guns for his twenty mill and letting them all go and shite and Siobhán looked at him and tutted and said it was a shame they were let say what they want in newspapers, there should be some kind of law about telling lies about people like that, and Mumbly Dave said Sure what lies, isn't it true that Johnsey's a bad yoke, sure look at him, he's the worst kind of a blackguard, he'd sell his granny to the highest bidder and Johnsey knew what that was — it was *sarcasm* — which Daddy had often told Mother was the *lowest form of wit.*

Sometimes it was hard to tell if someone was saying good things or bad things when there was *sarcasm* involved, but Johnsey was fairly sure that by calling him a blackguard and saying he'd sell his granny, Mumbly Dave was actually saying that the opposite was true and that all the stuff about him being a greedy divil and holding the poor developers over a barrel and destroying the whole village's future was lies. Why is it at all that things can't be said simple?

Siobhán said she had to go; she had to see about a job looking after an old couple in their house out towards Rooska, seeing as that fat cow was due back from her maternity leave in a few weeks. Mumbly Dave said Yerra Jaysus, she hadn't even been asked had she a mouth on her, and Johnsey jumped up from the edge of the couch and offered to make tea and cursed whatever slowness was in him that stopped him knowing to do these things without having to be told by Mumbly Dave. There wasn't as much as a barmbrack or a cut of tart in the house. Why had he to eat everything as soon as he got it? Should he offer her a proper drink? He said there was a bottle of red wine there if she'd like a glass, it wasn't in the fridge, though, and Mumbly Dave laughed all shrill like a little girl and looked at Siobhán and asked had she ever heard the bate of that? Red wine in the *fridge*, ha ha ha, and Johnsey thought again about the two rats who got on the finest until the girl rat came along and isn't it a fright to God to say a man could have violent thoughts about his only friend over a bit of a slagging that wouldn't cost him a thought normally, but delivered in front of Siobhán was like a stab into the heart?

Siobhán said she was grand, she'd have a drink the next time she called — the roads were crawling with guards lately. If she got this job looking after these two auld geriatrics in Rooska she could call loads, because it'd be on the road out. Mumbly Dave told her to call any time, as if it was up to him to be telling people to call to Johnsey's house. They walked her out to the gate and Mumbly Dave laughed at her car and called it a nun-mobile and Siobhán laughed as well and looked back at Mumbly Dave's yahoo car and said Little willy, big exhaust, and Mumbly Dave, who could talk a dead man back to life, just stood there with a wounded face on him and a fake smile painted across it, and Johnsey knew he was thinking about how Siobhán had probably actually seen his mickey inside in the hospital, and her slagging therefore had an edge to it like a new razor, and Johnsey caught himself enjoying Mumbly Dave's torment and felt ashamed. She wrote a number on a tissue from a plastic packet with a little black pencil that she had in her handbag and handed it to Johnsey and said Send me a text or whatever and we'll arrange something, and Johnsey took it and his hand was shaking a bit as he reached for it and he wondered did she notice the shake and if she did, did she know he was shaking with nerves just from being near her and did she think he was an awful weirdo?

Mumbly Dave was quiet for a while after Siobhán had gone. When he eventually came back around to being himself, he told Johnsey how Siobhán must have the hots for him big time. Why else would she have called to his house and gave him her phone number? You didn't see her calling to *his* house, did you? She didn't give *him* her number, written with an

185

eyebrow pencil, which every fucker knows is a way women have of telling a fella they want to ride them. Why would someone like Siobhán want to be hanging around with a fella like Johnsey? Mumbly Dave told him not to be thinking too much about her reasons — if you won the lottery would you ask the crowd above in Dublin what their reasons were for having a lottery in the first place? You would in your hole; you'd snatch the big cheque off of them, hand and all. A wan like Siobhán bothering with you without having to be begged — for a lad like you, that's like winning the lottery. Seeing as you're determined to refuse all them millions on offer from Herbie and the gang, you may as well take what's offered in other departments. Big land deal or no big land deal, you're still a farmer, kind of, anyway, and that counts for a lot with wans of a certain age and inclination. It's not your sultry good looks is after attracting her, that's for sure.

Mumbly Dave told Johnsey there was no sense trying to do a line with a girl in this day and age without a mobile phone. *Texts* are the new tool of seduction. And you, my friend, are a tool, he said, but not one skilled at seduction. You could have a wan all warmed up and gagging for action before you met her at all with a few nicely worded text messages. He said not to worry; he'd look after that side of things. You also need a couple of them nice shirts that you don't tuck into your pants. And pantses are out — you has to wear jeans, *boot cut* jeans — not them fuckin Lees or Wranglers from the eighties. And boots are out; you has to wear nice slip-on shoes. But not black ones, they has to be brown and pointy-looking. And you has to make your hair look as though you don't bother your hole combing it. And you can't be going around in a big puffy jacket with a hood or a duffel coat; you has to get a nice blazer or a leather jacket, but not one that looks new; like it has to *be* new but look old. And some lads only pulls their trousers halfway up their arses so you can see the tops of their jocks, but you had to wear right cool jocks in that case, with *Calvin Klein* written on them — the old three-pack Penneys Y-fronts wouldn't do. Yerra, forget about that anyway, you'd probably get bate up again if anyone saw you.

★ ★ ★

If Siobhán wanted to *arrange* something, like coming back to Johnsey's house without Mumbly Dave, and if she was going having a drink, and if she was worried about how the roads were crawling with guards lately, and if she lived miles and miles away, and if she was a saucy strap of a lady like Mumbly Dave said, then she could very easily have it in her mind to stay over in Johnsey's house for the whole night and God alone knows what else she might have inside in her mind. Imagine what Mumbly Dave would say if he knew about the thing with his mickey! It's possible for a thing to give you half of a horn and make you feel sick with worry at the same time just by thinking about it. What would Mother and Daddy think if Johnsey let sin happen under their roof? What would the spirits of his ancestors say to each other? The IRA great-uncles would probably be egging him on, seeing as they had to swear to God never to go near a woman the rest of their born days after they joined the priesthood. Daddy would probably say Well . . . good . . . man . . . Johnsey . . . begod. And Mother would slap him and tell him he was a fright to be praising the boy for being dirty and making a solid fool of himself.

He probably was going to make a fool of himself, in fairness. It was one thing to give every minute of the day thinking about how much you love a person and to have fine romantic thoughts when all you have to do is lie down like an old sheepdog and listen to their voice and sneak the odd look at them while they're foostering about with tablets and drips and sheets and what have you. It's another story to have to actually do things like give them something to eat and drink and decide how close beside them to sit and try to think of things to say and then to organize the words properly so that they come out through your mouth in the proper order and at a manageable speed. How is it you can't be given warning of things that's going to happen, like the newspaper bollix and the Unthanks being in the consortium and Siobhán arriving and making him sweat with delight and fear and desire and shame at allowing his friend to be hurt? How is it you can have no say in what happens you? Probably because he'd choose for nothing to ever happen him and he'd live out his days behind the window, looking out, wondering.

Mumbly Dave said if a woman wants you she'll ride you into submission. That's how women gets their way, apparently. Balls full, brain empty. Balls empty, you don't give a shite, anyway. But if you're going to be led around by your lad, it may as well be a flaker like Siobhán doing the leading. Johnsey didn't like that kind of talk about Siobhán. How would Mumbly Dave know anything about anything? All them auld stories about all the sex he'd had and all the other brilliant things he'd done were just made up. He was only raging that Siobhán had called to Johnsey and not down to the house Mumbly Dave lived in with his two brothers who he doesn't bother with on account of they're a pair of pricks and his father who goes every day to the pub and the bookies and pisses away what money he gets from the dole and what he can scrounge off of people and what Mumbly Dave's wrinkled, scrunched-up mother gets for cleaning the school and the few bits of offices below in the village belonging to the bigshots.

Isn't it a solid fright to say a man can have such mean auld thoughts about his only pal? He'd want to have a word with himself, in all fairness. How's it he couldn't keep a howlt on his own badness? He was turning into an awful bad yoke.

October

The milking would be getting light by October. You might be down to the one milking a day by then. Daddy wouldn't take his ease, though. He might do a third cut of silage, or he'd tighten up around the place in preparation for the winter, or he'd be still going off doing block-laying jobs. The cattle would go back in to the slatted house to shelter from the cold, and they wouldn't settle for ages but Mother would look in and say Ah, the auld dotes, come on now, auld dotes, curl up and be warm, and it was hard to believe when she talked like that to the cows that she had a tongue on her that could cut a man right in two.

Daddy used to love Halloween. He'd put tenpences into flour inside in a big pan and you had to try and get them out with your teeth, and if you did you could keep them. And he'd hang an apple off of a piece of string at the back kitchen door and you had to try and take a bite out of it with your hands tied behind your back and everyone would be roaring laughing. And he'd take Johnsey out around the yard and they'd both wear scary masks and Mother would let on to be frightened of them when they came to the kitchen window and Daddy would point up at the sky and say There's the witches, Johnsey! This is the only night they're allowed fly around on their broomsticks!

And you could nearly see the witches, soaring

around the moon, and hear them cackling, and the fear would feel lovely in your spine. And he'd make a big huge pantomime out of the cutting and eating of the barmbrack with the ring in it, saying the one to find the ring would have a long life and eternal luck, and it was always Johnsey that found it, and Johnsey could never know how Daddy made sure it was always him found it, but daddies know magic tricks that they're taught when their children are born and Johnsey wondered would he ever know them tricks.

* * *

Paddy Rourke shot Eugene Penrose in October. Then he went home and swallowed all his tablets together. He was on rakes of yokes for his heart and his bones and his liver and God only knows what else. Minnie Wiley found him in his bedroom. Minnie the Mouth, people called her. She used give Paddy a hand a few days a week to tighten up the place and do a few jobs, so she had her own key.

Men like Paddy should die noble deaths, like them Spartan fellas that fought the million Persians and saved the whole western world, or else they should live in health and happiness well beyond a hundred, and die in big, huge, comfortable beds, surrounded by crying women and strong, admiring men, looking at the ground to hide their tears and telling each other handed-down stories of feats of strength and bravery beyond words. But Paddy died alone in his cold old house, in a room that smelt like piss, with his pyjamas half off of him, covered in vomit.

★ ★ ★

Eugene Penrose had to have his left leg amputated. That means cut clean off. Paddy didn't go with the duck shot for a finish — he gave Eugene a barrel of heavy lead. The Unthanks beat Mumbly Dave up to the house to tell Johnsey about it. No one knew about poor Paddy at that stage; Minnie the Mouth hadn't yet found him in his stinking deathbed and run to tell every yapping auld biddy in the village about it. Mumbly Dave said later wasn't it a grand excuse for them two to stick their noses back in? Did he ask to know how is it they never told him they were in league with Herbie Grogan? Did he ask to know how was it they had the neck to face in to the hospital all them times to sit and bullshit about how great it was that all this building was to be starting up *mar dhea* they was only ordinary punters when all along they had every penny they had, and them two had a fair whack of shaggin pennies, have no fear, they had their Communion money, you can be guaranteed, stuck in with the rest of the bigshots that was trying to grab his land off of him? Johnsey knew Mumbly Dave was only put out he wasn't the one to tell Johnsey about Paddy shooting Eugene Penrose, but did he have to be so disrespectful? Johnsey still loved the Unthanks no matter what. Their shame pained him. What about it if they gave Herbert Grogan a few pound to invest for them? How's it he couldn't find words to comfort them?

Eugene was left bleeding on the hard ground in front of the pump for a good long while before help arrived. Mumbly Dave said he was nearly bled out before they scraped him up off of the road and put him into the ambulance and took him in to the hospital for the Paki doctors to sew him back together. Except they didn't — them boys'd sooner go chop-chop any day, Mumbly Dave said. They no like a sew, that for auld women. One leg plenty leg enough for bowsie white man. He only sit on hole watching telly, anyway. Johnsey didn't think that was how the Paki doctors talked. Doctor Frostyballs didn't, but he was Indian. Was it the same thing? God only knows. All them lads are much of a muchness, in fairness.

Eugene shouldn't have moved his headquarters from the IRA memorial. At least up there someone might have seen what was after happening and rang the ambulance quicker. No one knew it was Paddy did the shooting until the guards put the serial number from his gun into their computer and up popped Paddy's licence. The rat-faced townie lad who had kicked Johnsey in the head told the guards it was an auld boy did it, he stopped his car in the middle of the road and he put on his hazard lights, and he had white hair and mad eyes and he looked like the devil, and he walked around to the passenger side, and he waved on a couple of cars who had to go around him, and he took his time, and he took his shot, and Eugene went down screaming, and then he threw the gun in over the wall of the empty yard and got back into his auld Jetta and turned it around and fucked off back the way he came.

Jim Gildea the sergeant told Mary his wife who told everyone else that the townie lad had shat all over himself. The spread wasn't as wild as Paddy had planned for Johnsey with the duck shot, so Eugene Penrose took the whole blast. And while Eugene lay bleeding and screaming, the brave boy with the birds on his neck shat and pissed all over himself and cried like a little girl and for a finish one of the ambulance lads had to give him an injection to make him stop being such a stones.

Johnsey kept thinking about Eugene, lying on the road with the blood pumping out of him and his leg in bits. And then he'd think of Eugene when he was only a small boy in primary school, when they'd all been pals. The thoughts tormented him. Did Paddy shoot Eugene for *him?* Was it because Paddy had thought him too weak to take his own vengeance? Then he'd think of Paddy and all the times he'd patted him on the head with his big huge hand and smiled fondly at him when he was a child and how he used to think Paddy was like a mountain, dark and unmovable and eternal. But it turns out Paddy was like one of them mountains out foreign that are the same for years, and everyone thinks it's the finest, and they live along the side of it in green pastures as happy as Larry, and then all of a sudden one day the quiet mountain blows its top and explodes into the sky and pukes melted rocks all over itself and destroys anyone who can't run fast enough to the lowlands and finally the mountain destroys itself.

* * *

Mumbly Dave said there was more excitement in the village in the last few months than there was in a hundred years. If they won the county final, there wouldn't be as much of a hullabaloo. And it all boiled down to Johnsey Cunliffe. He was some troublemaker! What was he going to do next? Start a riot? Sure, he was fit for anything! Auld Peg-Leg Penrose is quare sorry he crossed you now, I'd say!

Sometimes if you're worried about a thing, it's great to have someone making a joke about it. Like when the curly fella in the newspaper said all them things about him, and Mumbly Dave gave that whole evening saying about how they should take the Land Rover to Dublin and wait for him outside his poncey office and they'd lamp the know-it-all arse off of him with hurleys and make him squeal like a fuckin cut pig. Johnsey nearly wet himself laughing the way Mumbly Dave described that, and all the laughing about it made it feel like the whole thing was only a joke and not really real. But Johnsey couldn't bear to listen to Mumbly Dave joking about Eugene Penrose and his leg. How's it he couldn't explain that to Mumbly Dave? How could he, when he couldn't explain it to himself?

Siobhán said when you lose a limb you end up

with too much blood. That can cause awful trouble for your heart because there does be too much pressure. That makes sense if you think about it — there aren't as many places for the blood to go. How is it though a human body knows how to make food into shite and drink into pee and a yoke you can't even see into a baby and your brain can do forty million things a minute according to that auld science teacher inside in the Tech and still it can't figure out it needs less blood if there's a bit chopped off of it? Worse again, Siobhán said sometimes people feel an itch where their leg or arm used to be, a *phantom* itch, like a ghost back to haunt them, and that itch can drive them right around the bend, because you can't scratch what's not really there. He remembered the itch under his cast inside in hospital and how that used drive him demented until Siobhán brought him in a knitting needle to poke down it for sweet relief and she told him not to let Sister or any of the other fatarses see him with it on account of they weren't meant to let people do that. He wondered had Eugene felt the phantom itch yet.

★ ★ ★

Aunty Theresa dragged poor Nonie and Frank up to the house not long after Paddy was buried. She wanted to know was he having an auction or what in the name of God was going to happen, and did he know that the rezoning wouldn't last forever, the farm would be only allowed to be a farm again before long and the show would be

196

over, and that nephew of Paddy Rourke's from England wouldn't be too happy with him for devaluing his inheritance with his quare notions and did he know there was such a thing as *compulsory purchase orders* and they'd soon get sick of him inside in the council and they'd *make* him sell and their idea of what's the going rate mightn't tally with what Master Johnsey Cunliffe had inside in his head and wasn't it a fright to God to say herself and Frank had to scrimp and scrape all their lives to get Susan and Small Frank through university and here was he sitting on several fortunes and acting like he was too good for them and Small Frank solid choked with asthma and he never lifting his nose from his books so that he may make something of his life and here was he going around making a show of them all with that waster of the Cullenses and he the talk of the whole country and poor Sarah hadn't a penny spare her whole life she didn't put into the Credit Union for *him* and now he wouldn't even look at his own aunty and she all that was left on this earth of his mother and why in the name of Jaysus would he not answer the phone?

Nonie said Ah now, ah now, but Theresa ignored her and Johnsey wondered had Theresa forgotten how Nonie was Mother's sister as well, and did she want him to sell the farm so he could give money to Susan and Small Frank who never once looked at him on the school bus and never once said a word when he was being tormented, only sat there smirking? Uncle Frank wanted to know was he doing a line with that little blonde nurse and he smiled and winked at Johnsey and Theresa told him shut his stupid face and she started *mar dhea* crying out of her with her hand on her forehead and Nonie went Ah now, again, and Frank threw his eyes towards heaven and looked fidgety and embarrassed and Johnsey remembered Daddy once saying how that poor fucker Frank made a hard bed for himself when he decided to take the free house and the big dowry and Mother said how dare he, her father paid no dowry to any man, Frank was picked from a long line of fine suitors, and Daddy looked at Johnsey and covered one side of his mouth and said you should have seen *that* line, Johnsey — a fairy, a blind man, a fella in his nineties, and Frank!

★   ★   ★

It was grand having Siobhán calling up all the same. You couldn't be giving the whole day to thinking about Paddy and Eugene and Theresa and people's expectations of you when you had to think about her calling up.

The next time she called after the time she showed up by surprise, they weren't even there. They'd been inside in the city, looking at hookers. Mumbly Dave had promised Johnsey he'd take him in to this street where they do be and he could have a look at his future wife ha ha ha! The hookers were quare-looking; a little fat lady who looked like a wan you'd see above at Mass only you could see half of her white belly because her top was too short and didn't meet

198

the top of her skirt. And there was a wan whose cheekbones looked like they could cut you. She was wearing a shiny tracksuit and her eyes looked dead. There was a skinny man with a thin moustache standing beside her who Mumbly Dave said was a woman and Johnsey couldn't believe it until he looked for a bit longer and then he could see that it really *was* a woman and Mumbly Dave said she was a mad bull-dyke pimp and Johnsey didn't know what them words meant but said nothing and Mumbly Dave said she'd cut your mickey off if you tried to get smart with her or the hookers, and while they were staring at her she clocked them and started walking towards Mumbly Dave's car and she had the head of a wan that'd take a bite out of you and eat you without salt and Mumbly Dave stalled the car in a panic and just as she got to them he got it going and she swung her foot at the car as they drove off and the hooker with the dead eyes only barely moved her head as they passed.

When they got back to the house, there were red words written on the kitchen window. Johnsey thought of them horror films he could only ever watch half of. Mumbly Dave told him it was lipstick. Lipstick, you dipstick! Ha ha ha! But Johnsey well knew Mumbly Dave was joking away his own hurt feelings. The words said:

Hi J
I called @ 6 but you must be off with your boyfriend
Txt me l8r 087 7946509
Siobhán xxx

Mumbly Dave said *Jay* like he was disgusted and *boyfriend* like he was more disgusted again and when Johnsey chanced a sideways look at him, he was nearly sure he saw a glint of water in his eye, but Mumbly Dave just said it was unbelievable that a fella could have rides of nurses scrawling love messages on his kitchen window and he not even having a phone to text her with and he having been given her number *twice* now and he was starting to wonder had he even a mickey to ride her with and it was an unnatural waste! If it was *him* she was after, he'd have had her rode and given the road long 'go but he had no farm of land ha ha ha and he'd want to be getting his finger out in the name of Jaysus. Johnsey couldn't stop looking at the lipstick message. Three kisses. Mumbly Dave said they could also stand for triple x, as in porno, like. Johnsey wished he'd stop saying words like hole and porno in regards to Siobhán, but how do you tell someone something like that without them thinking you're an awful holy Joe and an auld spoilsport and hurting them even further?

The next day they went into the phone shop and a wan who Mumbly Dave said had flaking knockers on her sold him a mobile phone and he couldn't tell what sort of knockers she had because he couldn't look at her, but she smelled quare nice and she sounded lovely and he dropped his money on the floor when he went to pay her and Mumbly Dave said Watch him, he's throwing it away, ha ha ha, signs on he can do it and he a feckin millionaire, ha ha ha, and

200

Johnsey felt himself going from red to purple and he suddenly pictured himself smashing the new phone into Mumbly Dave's face. How's it he couldn't just shut up and let him pay the girl besides trying to be smart the whole time and showing off and probably now the girl who smelled lovely would cop his face from the paper and think look at this greedy prick in buying phones and why is everything you do just so embarrassing and how is it he couldn't control them awful thoughts? Did badness now have the run of his brain?

Mumbly Dave said horse her off a text there so as they drove home. Johnsey asked him what should he say? Mumbly Dave said Jaysus boy, will I have to ride her for you as well? After he said that, Johnsey wouldn't please the prick and resolved to make his own text without any help. You had to *scroll* through the *menu* to figure out all the yokes but he didn't ask Mumbly Dave for his advice and he didn't make a bad fist of it all the same now and for a finish he said: *Hello Siobhán this is Johnsey Cunliffe sorry I missed you please call again.*

Mumbly Dave asked what was he after sending her? Had he the number in right? Johnsey wondered how Mumbly Dave was all of a sudden so browned off with him. It was *he* was making the smart comments and making little of Johnsey and yet here he was nearly shouting now about the blessed text and he was looking over at Johnsey and reaching to grab the phone off of him and the car was roaring for the want of a change of gear and he wasn't being too careful about staying inside the white line the way you have to be because Daddy always said to Mother when she was driving if you put your wheels out over the line, some day you'll go around a bend and there'll be as big a fool as you coming against you and BANG! Two dead fools. And no knowing how many crathurs of innocent passengers taken with them, all out of foolishness. And Mother would roar at him to shut his face but still and all she'd pull back towards the ditch to quieten him.

When Johnsey called out the text he'd typed, Mumbly Dave said hoo hoo hoo, that was the gayest thing he'd ever heard! Please call again? You're some tulip, boy! This is Johnsey Cunliffe! Mother. Of. Jaysus. You're some stones. You're . . . And the car shook as the wheels on Johnsey's side took too much of the soft verge and Mumbly Dave cursed and his hands moved fast on the wheel and when he got it straightened he said Ha ha! That shook you, boy! As much as to say he'd been doing the jackass on purpose, his bad driving only a stunt to put the wind up Johnsey. But there was a lot of colour gone from his face for a fella that was only playing the fool.

He must have copped on then that Johnsey was like a dog with him for making a laugh of his text to Siobhán and was wishing to God he could reach in to the sky and pull it back and send something else cool and smart and funny and imagine it was out there now, bouncing off of a satellite and back down to earth and into Siobhán's phone with the pink case around it and the blue love heart on it and wasn't it an awful dangerous thing, a text message, because once you pressed that little *send* button, that was it. Like pulling a trigger of a shotgun and sending a pellet into a little rabbit's brain as he sniffed the sweet spring air. You couldn't undo it. You couldn't ever take it back. Mumbly Dave said Don't worry, boy, don't worry, and drove straight and not too fast the rest of the road home.

★ ★ ★

It was all the one for a finish. Siobhán had no interest in big long text messages. She just said: *OK no prob Ill call 18r after wrk*. And that was it then, she would text that she was going to call and he would just reply *ok*, and she would arrive about six or half-six and one day she sent a text to say: *On way starving*, and he panicked and rang Mumbly Dave and asked what would he do and Mumbly Dave said he didn't know in the hell and he asked what had he in the fridge and Johnsey said sausages and rashers and puddings and he said make her a fry so I suppose and when Siobhán arrived she wanted to know did he really think she'd want to eat a plate of burnt, dead pig? And she laughed and told him eat it himself but it was quare hard to chew and swallow when your mouth was dry and your stomach was sick with embarrassment and she ate a sandwich made out of brown bread with cheese and sliced *apple*! Imagine that, a sandwich with *apple* in it! And after that if she said she'd be calling he'd have a bit to eat ready for her, like a sandwich made of brown bread and lettuce and low-fat cheese and a Diet Coke and an apple maybe (but not *in* the sandwich) because that's the kind of stuff women love eating, apparently.

Mumbly Dave took to going away before Siobhán arrived. If she sent a text message, he'd ask Johnsey what did it say and Johnsey would say she's calling in later and Mumbly Dave would nod his head and say nothing and then he'd say he had to go away, anyway, he was meeting a few of the lads in the village for a pint but Johnsey knew he was going to go home to watch *Home and Away* on his own and then probably *Emmerdale* and *Coronation Street*, maybe, with his mother because she was sometimes home by half-seven.

He was quieter these last few days since Siobhán started calling. He didn't ask Johnsey too much about what they did when she called. Johnsey thought that was strange, but in a way he was glad: how would he have told Mumbly Dave that he just sat there like a tool trying not to leave his eyes wander down her chest or up her leg, trying not to think about what happened in the hospital, listening to her giving out yards about auld Dinny Shanley trying to feel her arse all day and his wife dribbling all over herself inside in the bed? But still, all the same, wasn't it a fright that he couldn't have Mumbly Dave *and* Siobhán without having to feel guilty about Mumbly Dave feeling left out and then feeling resentful if he included himself and being scared in case Siobhán expected him to do or say something *meaningful* or what have you and was it an awful bad thing if he wished sometimes he could go back to walking down the Callows with Mumbly Dave and talking comfortable auld nonsense about nothing? It was grand having Siobhán calling up alright, but did one thing you had have to be a bit ruined by getting another thing? Is that how life balanced itself out?

How was he ever going to know what Siobhán wanted, anyway? She could talk away for hours and you'd still know nothing. Was it just the way he was on the road out to the Shanleys and it was handy for her to stop in to avoid going home too early to her mother who was a right sour-faced old trout of a wan by all accounts, forever giving out yards to Siobhán about being nowhere in life and her sisters were all married and settled down with lovely fellas, and if only Mammy knew the half of it, one of them was a rampant alcoholic and another was having an affair and her smarty-hole brother Peadair whose arse the sun shone out of was after failing all his exams above in UCD and Mammy after telling every auld witch in the parish that he was going to be the Attorney Fucking General! Or was Mumbly Dave right about her being one of them wans that goes mad for fellas with farms of land? What was so wrong about that, anyway? That hardly made her like the little fat lady with the short top or the dead-eyed girl in the shiny tracksuit, did it?

November

Halloween opened the gate to All Souls and then sure the next big push after that was Christmas. November would drag and you had to try not to think about Christmas or you'd go mad waiting for the time to pass. Wasn't Santy a great man all the same? He'd be flat out in November, so he would, making presents. They put up the decorations inside in town earlier and earlier every year. That's to try and drive people into buying stuff, Mother used to say. Imagine, All Souls just past, and feckin auld decorations up around the place. They should be banned from mentioning Christmas until halfway through December!

Some people offered up a sacrifice for the Faithful Departed in November. Mother said that was only auld shaping — them that went around spouting about giving up drink for the month were the same ones that would fill their auld faces and drink themselves stupid non-stop all December. Letting on to be holy. All they were doing was sparing up the money they'd piss away at Christmas.

* * *

There was another story in the newspaper about Johnsey in November. This time it was one of them papers that has pictures of women in only their knickers. He remembered once when he was a small boy, Mother caught him staring at one of them pictures with his mouth hanging open and she snatched the paper off of the table and rolled it up and went across to where Daddy was watching a match on the telly and she leathered him across the head with it and he got an awful drop because she had snuck up on him and she roared at him that she'd told him before about bringing that filth into the house and the child's mind would be poisoned. Johnsey burned with shame for being poisoned and getting Daddy into trouble and he worried that the poison from the picture had gotten into his mickey because it was trying to jump out of his underpants but he was afraid to ask Mother about it, the mood she was in.

This time, the newspaper only had a small picture of Johnsey, and it was the same one as last time — the one the posh lad's pal had taken of him real sneaky the time in the yard. But there was a big huge picture of Eugene Penrose, with a bandaged stump where his leg used be and he as white as a ghost, with a framed photograph in his hand of himself in his hurling togs from when he played under-sixteens before they gave him the road for being a bowsie. And above Eugene's photo, the big words said: LAND WARS.

And below them words, beside and below the picture of Eugene and his stump and his photograph were a load of words about Johnsey again and how 'the man who shot and almost killed Mr Penrose and later overdosed on prescription medication was closely linked with landowner John 'Johnsey' Cunliffe, who has come to national attention in recent weeks as a key figure in a massive land deal, reportedly demanding a twenty-million fixed reserve for a parcel of land central to local redevelopment', and Mumbly Dave said Yerra you're nearly as well off not bother reading it, and Siobhán said No, David, let him read it, he's not a baby, you can't be trying to protect him from the world, and Mumbly Dave said he wasn't, he was only trying to tell him that that sort of auld rubbish isn't worth reading and Siobhán tutted at Mumbly Dave and rolled her eyes and Johnsey saw her making faces across the room and Mumbly Dave was bright red and Johnsey wished he'd just start saying funny things again like the last time.

Eugene told the newspaper how everyone in his home parish blamed him for beating up Cunliffe even though he was never charged with that crime as there was no evidence against him and there was rakes of townies out around here now that had plenty of form for that sort of thing and Paddy Rourke had threatened him in the churchyard that he'd get his comeuppance and he had witnesses that would back that up, but he hadn't reported it at the time because he had great sympathy with the elderly on account of his own grandfather was old and infirm as well and he had had an awful dose of a childhood, with his father running off and his mother turning to the drink to console herself and he having been left to fend for himself. Mumbly Dave said auld Pissypants Patsy Penrose hadn't far to run, he was tapping Bridie Fitz below in the Munster pub when he wasn't inside in the bookies! But Siobhán shushed him before he could get going and he threw her an awful dirty look.

Eugene told how Johnsey had always acted like he was better than everyone on account he came from land and most other lads in their class were the sons of labourers and honest tradesmen and he always kept himself separate and signs on he was looking for all them millions to allow the development to go ahead, wasn't he convinced he had a divine right to be elevated above his fellow man? He wasn't saying John Cunliffe was behind his shooting, but he had an awful hold over people — there was plenty in the village at his beck and call, and since his parents had died, God rest them, he had lost the run of himself altogether. He was seldom seen in public but when he was, he'd walk over you. Whoever beat him up that time was probably at the end of their tether. Sometimes the have-nots lash out against the haves. That was a sad fact of life, brave Eugene said.

★　★　★

Mumbly Dave said Lookit, it could be worse — at least they're not making out you're a faggotyarse or a kiddyfiddler! Siobhán said Oh for God's sake, Dave, and rolled her eyes, but she was smiling as well, and they reminded Johnsey of Mother and Daddy when Mother used be trying to be cross with Daddy but she wouldn't be able. Why couldn't they all live there in the house together, and Johnsey could leave Mumbly Dave off with the big idea he was always talking about with the barn abroad and all the apartments you could put into it and the knobs from the city goes mad for them, we could call it The Barnyard or Cunliffe Manor or some shaggin thing and there'd be a rake of little Polish wans too, mad looking for Irish fellas, woo hoo boy we'd be right!

There was a big pile of money in the Credit Union and more in the bank; Aunty Theresa had straightened all that out for him and maybe she wasn't as bad of an auld boiler as she made herself out to be. Couldn't he at least sell a few sites and feck it to hell it wouldn't kill him to throw a few quid to Small Frank and Susan if that's what Aunty Theresa wanted and maybe he *was* being a rotten yoke, depriving all them people of work and money and opportunity and maybe then the Unthanks could stop feeling like they had to explain themselves but they weren't able and things would be easy and comfortable and lovely again in their warm kitchen with the smell of baking bread.

Isn't it a fright that Daddy or Mother couldn't have told him what he was to do after they died, before they died? Would Mother go mad with him if he had a woman living in the house? Would she think Mumbly Dave was very common and not a suitable pal? Would Daddy think he was an awful useless meely-mawly if he could make no fist of life at all? Would he be proud if Johnsey could tell the McDermotts to shove their lease and take back the land and tell the auctioneers and the consortium and the newspaper crowd to shove it all up their holes and let them all go and shite and if he married Siobhán and had a big dairy herd and a rake of children and while he was thinking all this an awful commotion had started abroad in the yard and when he looked out there was a wild-looking fella with black hair sticking up out of his head in tufts like a wet dog and he had a hurley and Mumbly Dave was standing in front of him pointing at his chest and Siobhán was saying Who the *fuck* is *that?*

★ ★ ★

It was Eugene Penrose's father. When Johnsey came out the door, he had leapt forward and swung a hurley and Mumbly Dave had ducked and grabbed him under the arms and he was roaring and screaming that Johnsey was going to go down for what he'd had done to his youngf'la and Johnsey never saw the other fella coming from the haggard wall who lamped him into the side of the head and as he hit the ground he saw the edges of Daddy's track and he thought to himself Mumbly Dave is going to catch that with his shoe now any second and all you could see was Mumbly Dave's arse and your man's boiling-red head like a twisted-around four-legged monster-man, roaring blue murder and swinging a hurley and Siobhán was screaming *Get away from him* and he realized someone was throwing kicks at him and when he looked up there was another monster, with two heads and two spare legs wrapped around its middle and one head had long blonde hair and it was biting the cheek off the other head with the black hair and it had drawn blood and the bitten head roared and the Unthanks' Bluebird swung in the gate and the squad behind them and the sudden storm stopped.

★　★　★

Siobhán had blood on her teeth. She was saying oh for *God's* sake, her *nails* were all broken! The guards had Patsy Penrose and Junior Penrose in the back of the squad. The Unthanks were standing in the yard, looking unsure of themselves. They'd seen Patsy and Junior heading off towards the Dark Road and they'd heard Patsy cursing Johnsey and knew well they were out to cause ructions and told Jim Gildea straight away. Jim wanted to know did they need an ambulance? Siobhán said it was grand, she was a nurse, she'd look after them, and sure no one was really injured. Mumbly Dave said Ambulance me hole, it's the fuckin *army* we need now, before some madman kills Johnsey, how's it ye can't arrest them cunts that writes lies in the newspapers about him, surely there's some law to say you can't blacken a man like that? The young garda who was with Jim told Mumbly Dave calm down but that only made him worse, and when he called the young garda a jumped-up little bollix, the garda pointed into his face and said Once more now, boy, and Mumbly Dave said And what? And what? And what? And luckily Jim Gildea came straight over and whatever else about Jim, Himself said afterwards, he was a long time at it and he knew how to douse a flame; he took the young lad away from Mumbly Dave and the Unthanks got Mumbly Dave to go inside and when they got in, Mumbly Dave turned on the Unthanks and called them a pair of fuckin Judases and asked why didn't they shag off back to their bigshot pals besides creeping around up here trying to brainwash Johnsey and Herself started to cry and so did Himself and Johnsey thought his heart would break in two.

★   ★   ★

That's a finish now to setting foot outside the gate any more. A man is only safe inside in himself. There's nothing people won't do or say when they think right is on their side. Who decides what's right? Is Mumbly Dave more right than the Unthanks because they had money given to Herbert Grogan and the developers and he hadn't? They could have had that done but years, before anyone had a notion *what* land would be rezoned. The clean truth unspoken became a lie, the way whatever unnoticed thing was inside in Daddy went bad and grew into a tumour that spread around his body and killed him. Maybe Mumbly Dave would have gave money towards this big plan too if he'd had a penny besides what you get for not working on account of your back being shagged or falling off of ladders and a nixer here and there and borrowing money off of the Credit Union below against this big payout that's meant to be coming from Timmy Shake Hands's insurance. That's a finish to it now, he wouldn't show his face any more and they could call him every kind of a blackguard all they wanted in words fancy or plain and God would have to get over him not going to Mass and the Unthanks could take their sorry eyes and their silence that was no longer easy but loaded up with the threat of apologies and excuses and leave him to his house and the odd walk down the river field to the Callows and if the world wanted him for something they could come and ask politely and he'd tell the world politely to go way and have a shite.

If them two detectives from inside in town ever came back promising justice would be done or asking if he knew anything about what Paddy done, with Jim Gildea behind them looking down at his shoes and trying to remember every detail to take home to Mary, he'd give them no hop. If any more business people arrived up with their Alsatian smiles and their auld spiel about deeds or deals or private treaties or what have you, he'd run them. He'd pull the phone from the wall altogether: no more of that auld craic. He wondered would Siobhán still want to call in and talk about the Shanleys and her mother being an awful wagon and her sisters being a smug pair of bitches and eat her apple sandwiches now that she'd had to bite a lad's face to stop him being killed? Would she say Ah here, this lad is too much hassle for too little in the way of bravery or looks or charm or dates in big restaurants where foreign fellas with tea towels on their arms comes over to put salt on your chips for you? Would Mumbly Dave find a new friend who wouldn't have poison thoughts about him every time he cracked a joke in front of a girl who had no more interest in him in a romantic way than in the man in the moon? There's too many things in the world that can go wrong. There's too many *variables*, that science teacher would have said. And even if you could catch all them auld variables in time, before they ballsed things up on you, everything would go bad for a finish, anyway. Interfered with or left alone, everything eventually turns rotten and dies.

★ ★ ★

Isn't it a pure balls, Mumbly Dave said, that a man could have such luck and to have nothing only misery come of it? He used to think Johnsey was mad to be humming and hawing about selling the land, but now he knew what it really was: Johnsey had *loyalty*. Why else would he defend the Unthanks, and they feeding him with one hand and trying to pull out his guts with the other? It's a great quality in a man. He was loyal to his family, even though they were all gone from him. He wouldn't sell the land that kept them. He wouldn't allow concrete to be poured on their years of toil. He could see past big auld plans for cinemas and shops and matchbox houses, and sure who'd benefit in the long run

215

only the same few fat fuckers that was running the show all along and making pure-solid fools of the whole country? It'll all come out some day, boy, that you was the only one to call a halt to all the auld grabbing and greed and that no money would pay you to sell out your auld home.

Siobhán said nothing, only bit back her broken nails and filed them with her elbow sawing madly back and forth and tutted and cursed those stupid inbred *rednecks* and the anger sparked off of her and it was impossible to know was she cross with the Penroses or the newspaper or Johnsey himself for causing so much upset just by being alive. It was hard to figure *anything* out about Siobhán, in all fairness. She was an unknowable thing, a solid mystery, like the black pool above on the side of Ton Tenna that Daddy said goes the whole way down to the centre of the earth and if you gave a few seconds looking at it you wouldn't be able to turn your eyes away from its still darkness and you'd feel a mad attraction to it even though it struck terror into your heart and before you knew it Daddy would be saying Come on will you, what the hell are you at, and he'd have found the auld wandering heifer for the old boy who'd rang him for a digout and twenty minutes would have passed.

*   *   *

Siobhán said he'd be an island of grass for a finish. The sudden way she spoke and the words she used made his brain stall for a few seconds

216

and his heart jump. They'll just build around you, love. And she moved over to his end of the long couch and put her hand on his forehead and ran her fingers back through his hair that he should have gotten cut ages ago but it's quare hard to sit in that chair below in the barbers when that lady that works there now is pushing her big chest into the back of your head and you're afraid to look into the mirror even in case she thinks you're staring at her and you're praying to God you don't strike a horn and you know your face is gone purple and all she wants to know is are you going on any holidays. Auld Mugsy Foley never gave one shite where you were going on your holidays once you sat down and shut up and listened to him telling you what he'd do if *he* was the Tipp manager while he sheared your head clean of hair. Johnsey could see Mumbly Dave was watching all this and he wondered did Mumbly Dave think he was a right baby for getting knocked so easy and being saved by a girl from Junior Penrose's boots while Mumbly Dave fought like a lion to keep Patsy Penrose from lamping him with his hurley? Did he even say thanks to Mumbly Dave? What was wrong with him at all? Where were the words in him?

Love, she called him. But sure, in all fairness, that auld wan that used come around with the breakfasts and the lunches and the dinners inside in the hospital used call *everyone* love. She even called Doctor Frostyballs it one day. She banged her trolley into the backs of his legs as he stood beside Johnsey's bed and said Oh sorry, looove, and she winked at Johnsey as much as to say she wasn't sorry at all, really, and Doctor Frostyballs only looked at her down his brown nose and barely moved for her. All them townie wans calls everyone love. But Siobhán wasn't exactly a townie wan; she came from a big house out towards Clonbrien that Mumbly Dave showed him one day and he'd felt like a right sneak going out there at all to stare in through a row of trees at Siobhán's home but he couldn't stop himself imagining her bed inside in that big house, covered in the smell of her, and all her girly things lying around, and drawers full of mysterious, delicate, frilly things! Would he ever see that room for real? What would he even do in there, besides creep around like a sneak? It'd be like putting a shit in a perfume bottle, leaving the likes of him in there.

Mumbly Dave said he'd head away and leave them at it but Siobhán said they weren't *at* anything, he had an awful cheek, but Mumbly Dave didn't laugh, only stood at the door with a puss on him. She told him he couldn't be going down around the village when all the *peasants* were so riled up — they'd be out around the place with torches and pitchforks next! But Mumbly Dave said he wasn't afraid of the Penroses or anyone else, and he was used to ignoramuses giving him abuse, sure you had to grow a thick skin to be pals with *that* fella, and he cocked his thumb towards Johnsey and it was only then that Johnsey realized how easy it had been for him to sit up here like a gom, waiting to be entertained and carted around the country and told stories and shown hookers and saved from misery, and not once did he say thanks to Mumbly Dave for anything or even offer him a few bob for petrol for his yahoo car. He said Please don't go 'way, Dave, and Mumbly Dave looked a bit embarrassed but he said Grand so, and he sat back down near the window like a soldier on guard duty and Siobhán stayed running her hand through Johnsey's hair and once or twice she kissed his shoulder and the awful heaviness he'd had in his stomach since the Unthanks left with their tears began to lighten and Mumbly Dave started telling about the smell off of Pissypants Patsy Penrose's underarms and how he thought there was creatures living under there as yet unknown to science.

★　★　★

Siobhán said no more about him becoming an island of grass nor gave any opinion about the land again, only called in as usual and ate her quare sandwiches and Mumbly Dave started to stay when she called and that bit of crossness that had been between them for a while melted away like spring hailstones in the yard. Johnsey stopped feeling that stupid jealousy like he owned her and even when one day she leaned right over to get her fags out of her handbag and Mumbly Dave made a shape like he was *mar dhea* going to slap her arse, and he winked over at Johnsey with that old wicked smirk, he was able to smile back and laugh so that Siobhán straightened up and caught him and said What are you laughing at, and she swung around and caught Mumbly Dave smirking out of him and she knew well he was at devilment and she called him an ignorant bogtrotter and he called her a snobby auld bitch and Johnsey wondered how was it *he* couldn't say them things like Mumbly Dave and make Siobhán open her eyes wide and cover her mouth as if to say she couldn't believe her ears and laugh and slap him on the arm and just be easy and funny and normal. Why was he such an oddball?

December

Who's to say a man and a woman has to do certain things in a particular order? Do you have to first meet and then go around together for a while and hold hands and kiss and then get engaged and get married and build a house and have children and live out your days as snug as bugs? Sure that's nearly all done away with now, surely, that holy sequence that meant you were respectable and doing things right opposite the neighbours and God. People have *unconventional* relationships these days. You'd hear talk on the radio about men marrying men and women marrying women and men and women not marrying each other at all, only living together in the one house and sure what about it? Our Lord surely had bigger fish to fry these days besides going around worrying about who was doing what in bed with who, what with all them madmen going around trying to kill everyone in His name.

There was no point in thinking too much about Siobhán or what she wanted, or if she wanted anything other than someone to listen to her giving out while she ate her sandwiches. If something is meant to be, it's meant to be. Is that really true, though? If it is, couldn't you do anything you wanted and never be held accountable? You'd just say Jaysus sorry about that, but it was meant to be, don't you know we're all slaves to fortune? Like them Punch and Judy puppets that used be pucking the heads off of each other inside in their little tent in Dromineer on summer Sundays. A fella with ropey hair and a girl with long dark hair and blackness in her eyes and sandals on her feet controlled them and if you saw her before the show all you could think about was her, unseen inside in that little tent and the darkness and the beauty and the mystery of her. And no matter how you screamed and roared at the puppets to watch out, the same thing would happen every single time. The ropey-hair fella and the dark girl controlled everything, like two gods, and they wouldn't be swayed from their course by a flock of screeching children.

★　★　★

Mumbly Dave started to do a line with a girl from the city. Woo hoo, boy, I'll be right for the Christmas, lads! This wan is mad for me! Siobhán would smile at him and look at Johnsey and roll her eyes to heaven and Mumbly Dave would be hunched over his mobile and he'd be click-click-clicking away ninety and smiling to himself and he'd laugh now and again, high and giggly, like a woman. He'd met this wan while he was doing a bit of tiling inside in a school. She was a *teacher*, imagine! He had to be quare careful about the nixers these days, auld Timmy Shake Hands was mad trying to catch him out. Wouldn't you think the prick would leave it go; it wasn't out of his pocket the claim was coming. It was the insurance company would be paying out. What odds to Timmy, in all fairness? The bitter auld bollix.

Siobhán kept asking when would they get to meet her, this big love of Dave's? Was she one of these smart city ones that think they'll spontaneously combust if they come too far out from town? What does she teach, anyway? Braille? And Johnsey was glad that he got it straight away — she was saying your wan must be blind to like Mumbly Dave — but Mumbly Dave had to think about it for a few seconds, and he spent the few seconds looking out of his mouth at Siobhán and then said Oh ya, ha ha ha. But there was no laughter in his eyes, and Johnsey was pure-solid ashamed for egging her on inside in his head to make little of Mumbly Dave. What kind of a fella *wants* his friend's feelings to be hurt?

★　★　★

Mumbly Dave loved him. He knew it before Siobhán said it, but didn't know he knew it. How's it he couldn't live up to it? It's an awful burden, being loved. Even by a little fat man. Imagine if Siobhán loved him. He'd never cope with that. That was a worry to join the rest of his worries inside in the room in his brain where he tried to keep them all together with the door locked on them. It was no good, though, they squeezed through the keyhole and flowed out through the jambs and took their shape again outside like the yoke in *Terminator 2* that was

223

made of liquid and could become anything it
wanted and could sneak around the place letting
on to be a puddle and all of a sudden it'd be
running around stabbing people. Paddy Rourke
was in that room, and Eugene Penrose and his
stump and the Unthanks and Aunty Theresa and
the newspaper people who thought he was a
woeful bollix and the neighbours who thought he
was a rotten greedy fecker and the whole village
who blamed him for calling a halt to progress
and Mother and Daddy, both dead and he never
having done one thing his whole life they could
boast about and it'd soon be Christmas and
should he buy a present for Siobhán? And if he
even managed to walk in the door of one of them
girly shops inside in town and the girl asked him
who was the present for, what would he say? A
nurse who gave me a handjob one time and now
comes to my house to eat sandwiches and give
out?

People can be an awful dose. If you only had
to look at them on television, everything would
be grand. When they wanted to buy your father's
land and say things about you in newspapers and
make little of you below in the village and be
your friend and be your nearly girlfriend and
shoot lads over what they done to you or really
over what was done to them and look out of their
mouths at you for a reaction or an answer or a
laugh or a digout or an action of which you're
not capable in a million years, they'd wear you
out. They'd go through you for a shortcut.
They'd wreck your head, the townie lads would
say. Isn't it a noble thing all the same, loneliness?

There's dignity in it, at least. You can't make a show of yourself when you're on your own. You can't sound stupid opposite nobody. People are better inside in your head. When you're longing for them, they're perfect.

★   ★   ★

That auld crossness came back around the start of December. Siobhán said to Johnsey that Mumbly Dave was only a user. Mumbly Dave said Siobhán was only teasing him. Siobhán said Mumbly Dave was a right weirdo. Imagine, a man in his thirties hanging around with young fellas, driving around in his Johnny-go-fast car, with everyone laughing at him! Mumbly Dave said you'd be as well off give that wan the road, I'm only saying it for your own good, she's waiting until you haven't a drop of blood left in your brain because it's all holding up your horn and you'll ask her to marry you and she'll bleed you dry. Siobhán said she couldn't believe that thing with Mumbly Dave and the barn and he'd make some balls of that job and leave you in the shit, don't even dream of it, no one would want to live in a crappy apartment in a smelly old cowshed. Mumbly Dave said she only wants you selling everything up so she can give the rest of her days going out foreign and buying expensive shite inside in Brown Thomas like all them wans that thinks they're bigshots. Siobhán said Mumbly Dave was probably a closet gay. Mumbly Dave said Siobhán was a sneaky little bitch. Then he got kind of sorry and said Yerra lookit, women don't be in their right mind half the time, with their periods and what have you.

He wasn't even sure when they had started to read each other so violently behind each other's backs. It sort of built up over a couple of weeks: a little dig laughed off was brought up when the digger was gone; a smart comment ignored at the time was repeated indignantly when the commenter was in the toilet. They started to change the air when they shared a room. They made it harder to breathe: you'd be aware of your lungs filling and emptying and you'd try not to make noises breathing because that drove Siobhán mad and she'd want to know why you sounded like a fucking respirator and Mumbly Dave would say Leave the man breathe any way he wants, and she'd say Mind your own business, and he'd say it *was* his business if she was tormenting his friend and she'd say Oh really? And he'd say Yes really. And she'd take a pull of her fag and blow the smoke hard in his direction and he'd tell her she was a classy bird all right and she'd say Are you still here, David? Have you not got a hot date? And she'd make that snorting noise at the back of her nose like she thought he was no more going on a date that night than the man in the moon and he'd say I have actually, and she'd say You'd better run along so, and he'd say I'll see you, Johnsey, and Johnsey would only say See you, and he never even got up off of his hole to walk as far as the yard with him any more, only sat looking at Siobhán and smelling her and hating himself. Mumbly Dave said he was *pussy-whipped*. What

226

the hell did that mean? It was some kind of a weakness, like some kind of a sex thing that only a fool would get involved in.

If he couldn't ask Mumbly Dave what he should buy Siobhán for Christmas, who could he ask? He knew if he went down to the bakery the Unthanks would give a whole hour at least talking about it with him. Himself would suggest something silly like a pound of sausages and Herself would tell him don't be daft and she'd laugh and he'd laugh and nudge Johnsey when she wasn't looking and they'd warm him with smiles and fill him with fresh bread and buns and tea. But he'd be afraid then they'd want to tell him they were sorry they hadn't told him about the consortium and he'd say it was grand, what about it, weren't they perfectly entitled? And they'd say about how they didn't know what way it would work out and it was no treachery and Jackie knew all about it. And what if he started crying like an eejit? It'd be out of sadness over their sadness and the mention of Daddy, but it'd only make everything worse, and Herself would start crying again and she'd stand at the sink, knotting a tea towel in her soft old hands, saying *everyone* invested with them, Johnsey, *everyone* thought it was a great idea, *everyone* . . .

★　★　★

Siobhán said they were going to go out properly at Christmas. She hadn't had a proper night out since her going-away do with the fatarses from

227

the hospital. And that was crap, because only three of them came and they were as dry as shites. They talked about *babies* all night! Who wants to spend a whole night out talking about *babies?* God, like. Two fellas come over at one stage and they were *really* funny, and one of them, God he was *gas*, was messing around and he just rubbed his hand sort of by accident really off one of their arses and she screeched like a banshee and the bouncer came over and told the fellas to get out and like, so what if he *did* feel her arse, he was a *fella*, that's what they *do*, he wasn't trying to *rape* the silly bitch and she should have been grateful, anyway, that *anyone* wanted to put their hand on her scabby old arse, never mind a ride of a fella. God, like.

Johnsey pictured himself grabbing that ride of a fella's hand and twisting it around until his wrist snapped like a dry twig and he went off bawling like a child with a kicked arse for himself and his hand on backwards and he wouldn't be so funny then, he wouldn't be the big gas man then, over talking smart to girls and taking liberties and thinking he was God's gift. Johnsey would put manners on him.

No he wouldn't. He wouldn't say a word to him. If he was ever in a pub or a disco or one of them places with Siobhán and some smartyhole came over all auld chat and was trying to get off with her, what would he do? Probably he'd stand up like an eejit and get redder and redder until someone asked him was he okay and the smartyhole would look at him and smirk and Siobhán would roll her eyes in crossness and the smartyhole fella would smirk back at her and she'd get thick with him for leaving her down opposite people and looking like a lunatic and what the hell was *wrong* with him, anyway, she was only *talking* for God's sake. Maybe if Mumbly Dave was there as well with his teacher wan it'd be okay because Mumbly Dave would be able to say something smart to your man and make little of him and sure in all fairness if they were all out together they'd be like proper people on a night out and no one would be over schmoozing with Siobhán and being gas and making her laugh the way he wasn't able to.

Siobhán wanted to go in to this restaurant in the city. They have a mural downstairs of Venice, and you can sit in this corner, surrounded by the mural, and it's nearly like *being* in Venice! And they do the *nicest* carbonara you ever tasted. What the hell was carbonara? How would he order something that was wrote down in a foreign language? Probably he'd ask for something and he'd think he was saying it right but the waiter wouldn't be able to make out what he was saying and he'd say Pardon me, sir, and Johnsey would have to say it again, and your man still wouldn't hear him and he'd be kind of smiling at him and he'd lean his Italian ear right in to Johnsey's mouth and he'd accidentally roar it out into his ear and your man would jump back and look frightened of him and people at other tables would stare over and your man would say That's not a main course, sir, it's a type of ice cream, and he'd snigger and Siobhán would laugh and people at other tables would laugh as well and shake their heads, and he'd wish he'd done away with his stupid self while he'd had the impetus that time.

* * *

The big fight happened on the second-last Friday before Christmas. Siobhán told him to text Mumbly Dave and ask him to know would he bring the teacher wan up to the house so they could have a look at her. She said she was in no rush home; she could even stay over if they had a drink. It was Friday night, for God's sake. They were staring Christmas in the face! She couldn't stay in one of those creepy rooms on her own, though; she'd have to sleep in with him. Aw, she said, am I after embarrassing you love? Don't worry, I won't jump on you! I hope you have fresh sheets on your bed! He hadn't changed them in weeks and weeks. Christ. Balls. Then she said she was going to run down to the off-licence and would she bring back a Chinese and he said Grand, and she said What will you have, and he said Beef curry and chips, and she said *Typical man* and laughed but it was a nice laugh and thank Christ, now he'd be able to change the sheets and tighten up the room above and hide Dwyer's magazine.

She was going to stay the night. In his bed. Oh, Lord. Would she be in her knickers or what? He horsed a shovel of coal and two logs into the fire. Imagine if the back boiler broke. She'd want about five blankets. Or she mightn't stay at all in the cold. Oh, Mother of Christ. An actual girl, in his bed.

Will u call up 2 nite he sent Mumbly Dave.

Im goin to town u sir Mumbly Dave sent back straight away.

Bring ur 1 back here n stay over. He had that idea himself. How's it he'd never thought before of asking Mumbly Dave did he want to stay? Himself and the teacher wan could easily sleep in the big double bed in the spare room. It had hardly been used since the Yanks stayed that time. He'd put fresh sheets on that bed too. He was starting to feel a bit excited. He was having a few people around. He was throwing a party. He was entertaining. He was in his hole. He was doing what he was told.

OK sound said Mumbly Dave. Still and all, though, it was going to be great craic. Mumbly Dave and Siobhán would have to call a halt to that auld sniping with your wan around. Mumbly Dave would be as high as a kite, trying to make *two* women laugh. All Johnsey'd have to do would be laugh. He could worry about the sleeping part after. There was no point thinking about it. That kind of thing all comes natural, anyway. That's what Daddy said one time abroad in the yard when Mother told him he had to have a talk with the boy about the facts of life. He'd heard Mother telling him in the back kitchen: You have to, Jackie. He can't be going around like a gom, not knowing what does what. But Daddy didn't want to, he said Yerra them teachers tells them all that stuff these days.

Mother said They do in their arses, now tell him what's what and be done with it. Daddy said how no one had had to feckin tell *him*. Signs on, Mother said. For a finish, Daddy turned around to him at the milking-parlour door and said Don't worry about all that auld craic with women and sex and what have you, that all comes natural. All right? Grand. Good man. Come on so till we get these cows milked.

★ ★ ★

Siobhán arrived and backed her car right up to the front door. She had the world of drink inside in the boot. They ate their Chinese fine and quick and she drank a glass of wine with hers and he drank a can of Harp with his. Then he threw the dishes into the sink and started to tighten up a bit. Siobhán said he was some fusspot; it was only Mumbly Dave and some slapper that was coming, not the pope and the queen. But before she could finish, Mumbly Dave drove in to the yard and she skipped over to the window and looked out and said Aw for fuck's sake, where *is* she? Either she's a dwarf or he hasn't brought her. Ah shit, anyway! We have to listen to Mumbly Dave for the night for nothing!

And he came in with a bag of drink and told them how Evelyn couldn't come on account she had to take the kids on a school tour early in the morning and she had to have an early night and Siobhán said Really, Dave? Is that really true? About *Evelyn?* And the way he went red gave the game away. You wouldn't get much past her. Why would you make up a girlfriend, Dave? You *weirdo?*

Johnsey didn't think Mumbly Dave was a weirdo. So what if he tried to embellish himself a bit? Plenty did it. He'd imagined himself being more than he was and having more than he had every day of his life. Mumbly Dave's face was getting redder and redder and Siobhán should have let it go and left him make a laugh of himself and he'd have had a funny way surely of explaining why he invented a woman for himself inside in town and it'd seem like a gas thing he'd done and nothing out of the ordinary at all, only a bit of fooling around. But she kept staring at him and shaking her head and saying he was an awful weirdo and Mumbly Dave for a finish got pure thick and said he'd done it to have an excuse not to be knocking around up here while *she* was around the place, and Siobhán said Oh, so it's *my* fault you're a fucking freak? And Mumbly Dave said she was a poison bitch and a gold-digger and he was the one that was here all along helping Johnsey through all his trouble.

Siobhán said Really? What did you do to help? Besides slug cans of beer and talk bollocks to him about all the imaginary women you've had sex with?

And Mumbly Dave said I writ a letter to them newspapers.

And Siobhán, all sarcastic, said Wow! That was some letter I'd say! What did you say to them?

That they was only a shower of shitbags, all a them newspaper fellas, and they didn't know notten about Johnsey Cunliffe and . . .

Dear Newspaper Fellas, You is only a shower of shitbags. Wow, Dave! I can't believe you didn't make the front page. It's a wonder they haven't been on to you to know would you be their new editor-in-chief.

I still done more than you, up here tormenting the poor boy with your tits inside in his face, making a pure fool out of him.

You're a horrible jealous yoke. That's all you are. You fairly latched on to Johnsey because you had no one else and he's too nice to get rid of you. You're a big, fat, friendless loser, Dave. That's all you are. Why don't you go back down to your council hovel and ride your sister or whatever it is ye do for fun down there? You *freak*.

Mumbly Dave had no answer. Or if he did, he hadn't the stomach for the saying of it. He looked at Johnsey and there was a big fat tear rolling slowly down his cheek and it flung itself on to the floor and Johnsey turned his face away from Mumbly Dave and stared at the little star-shaped puddle that the tear made and when he looked up again, his friend was gone.

★ ★ ★

It was Minnie the Mouth who came to the door the next day to tell Johnsey the news. Sure, why wouldn't it have been? She fattened on the telling of sorrowful tales, and everyone has to take their pleasure where they can. Minnie the Mouth said wasn't he a pal of yours, that boy of the Cullenses? Her eyes were gleaming. Her cheeks were glowing red with excitement. She was trying to see past him to know who had he inside. Did you not hear the news? Well, I'm fierce sorry now to be the bearer of sorrow, but it looks like he was killed last night. Lord have mercy on him. Apparently he slid on black ice and hit that feckin auld dead elm at the bad bend over beyond near Pike's Cross. In the small hours of this morning it was. Where the hell was he off to, I d'know? How well he had to hit the tree! By all accounts he was killed outright, at least there's that, anyway. That boy always drove like the divil; I always maintained he was an accident waiting to happen. At least there was no one took with him! He was often up here with you, wasn't he? Ye palled around a lot, didn't ye? He thought the world of you, I'd say. I often heard him backing you up to the hilt and you getting read left, right and centre below in the village by them that knows notten. I seen ye knocking around together. That auld bad bend is a solid fright. Lord save us and guard us, isn't it just a fright to God? They'll surely straighten it now. Or drag out that auld tree out of it at least. The poor misfortune, how well he had to hit the tree.

★　★　★

There was only three or four lumps of coal in the bucket by the fire, and nare a log. How's it he never thought to fill the log box to the top and bring in a couple of buckets of coal while he was

235

at it? Daddy always had a plot of turf in the bog out towards Cloughjordan. Your back'd be broke turning and footing and bagging and piling it on the trailer and dragging back all the miles home with your wobbly load and then lugging the bags into the shed and emptying them and stacking the turf up nice, but it saved you burning too much coal when winter came. Coal goes in and gets red-hot real fast and burns itself out in no time. It's brilliant while it lasts, but it never lasts long. Turf burns gentler and lasts longer. He'd ring your man in Clough in the spring and see about getting a plot again. How hard could it be? Surely be to God he could organize something as simple as that. He'd book the plot and your man would ring when the turf was cut and ready to be turned and he'd give it a few days and he'd foot it and Siobhán could give a hand if she wanted but she probably wouldn't in fairness, young wans would hardly choose to give summer days to breaking their backs in the bog.

Siobhán kept saying Oh my *God*, oh my *God*, oh my *God*.

Yerra shut your face, he felt like telling her. Just shut your face. If you hadn't made little of him none of it would have happened. He'd never say that out, though. You're as well off keep your powder dry when you're that cross, for fear you'd say things you can't take back. Anyway, it was *he* was responsible. Women can't help rising rows. He was here like a prick looking out of his mouth at Siobhán and grinning at her like a fool while she danced around the kitchen to the radio and drank vodka with Coca-Cola in it and

236

smoked fag after fag and told him he was very *closed off*, he was very *mysterious*, he was very *deep*, not like them *dicks* inside in town. And he lapping it up like an auld hungry dog getting fed scraps while his only pal drove around the countryside in pure-solid temper and finished up making bits of himself.

Did it take him long to die? Was he panicking and shaking and trying to draw air into his bursted lungs? People always say people in accidents were killed outright, but you knew half the time that was only as comfort for them that's left behind. How did anyone ever know? Maybe Mumbly Dave sat strapped in to his yahoo car, still with all his senses while his insides bled, thinking about how Johnsey had let Siobhán say all them things and how his pal had turned his face away from him and never even tried to defend him or stop him from leaving.

He'd lain in his bed chancing the odd look over at Siobhán who snored like them auld fellas that used be in Daddy's ward inside in the hospital. She never even went near his mickey. He'd seen her in her knickers, though, at least, as she hopped into the bed. They were light blue with white frilly bits at the edges. She'd kissed him once on the lips and said You're *lovely*, forget about Dave, he'll be grand, he has a hide like a rhino, and she smelt like fags and liquor and perfume and she turned away and fell asleep and she took all the duvet and most of the mattress and he lay there like a gom with his arse hanging out over the edge of the bed, trying to keep his horn from poking into her. And at some

237

stage while he was doing that, imagine, Mumbly Dave met his lonely death.

* * *

Not long after Siobhán had left, Dermot McDermott had come to the door. Johnsey spotted him over the haggard wall from the room above, where he'd been smelling Siobhán off of a pillow and starting to get sorry about leaving her go like that, in a wicked temper with tears in her eyes. He'd told her he'd sooner be on his own and when she went to give him a hug he'd pulled back from her and she said Oh right, be that way, so. *I'll* miss him too, you know. You will in your arse, he thought. Or did he say that out loud? It was hard to know. Whichever, she'd fecked off, in a right auld strop for herself.

Johnsey had the Winchester down from the attic before Dermot McDermott made it across the yard and up to the front door. It felt cool to touch and its heaviness was like an anchor. It fit lovely in to his shoulder, like it was made especially for him. He hadn't picked it up since that February day long ago. When he got as far as the kitchen, Dermot McDermott was looking in the window with his hands cupped around his eyes. There was an envelope or something in one of his hands. Johnsey stayed by the door where he couldn't be seen. Dermot McDermott walked back along the yard and looked up at the gap between the slatted house and the near shed out to the big yard. Then he started back towards the house. Johnsey drew the sight on him, so that his curly, cute hoor's head sat bobbing on the bead, getting bigger and bigger as he progressed towards the window.

Johnsey felt the power of death over life, just like your man in that song about the fella that accidentally on purpose killed the lone rider. How a thing as small as a tightening in a muscle in your finger can do a thing so big! He'd never do it, though. But it was no harm to have a weapon close at hand in this day and age. It's funny how he'd never thought of keeping it close before. Maybe a shock like he'd gotten brings clarity to the mind. If them boys that went at Paddy that time ever rolled into the yard, or if them ratty-faced lads from the newspapers ever came back around the place, or any of the Penroses, he'd lose valuable minutes running upstairs and foostering about with the attic door and putting in the cartridges. Best to keep it downstairs for good.

★　★　★

Now there was a quare fella abroad at the gate and every now and again he'd lean in around so Johnsey was able to just about see him and he'd roar into a bullhorn. He sounded like the same lad who'd rang his mobile earlier. How had they his number? When it had rang, he'd thought it was Mumbly Dave. Imagine if it was! Well, youssir, bejaysus it's grand up here, your father said to tell you stop acting the bollix and put away his gun before you hurt yourself. And your mother says You're a dirty scut for letting that little strap sleep inside in your bed with you. Your mother says she's an awful trollop, that lady! Not *my* words! Don't worry, youssir, it wasn't your fault. Once that wan got her claws in I was back to having notten, anyway. Hadn't we some craic, though, for a while? Don't worry, boy, no one blames you for notten. All you are is a victim of circumstance.

But it was a lad he didn't know and he had one of them quare accents and he was talking all friendly but the way his words were coming out put Johnsey in mind of a fella in one of them plays they put on sometimes inside in town in the Scouts' hall, like the words was all wrote down by someone else and learnt off by heart but the sayer of the words was meant to convince the hearer of them that they were his own, and for a finish he must have gotten sick of getting back nothing only silence and he said I'm going to pass the phone now to someone who's worried about you and just wants to see that you're okay. Okay? Okay.

And it was Himself and he sounded slower and quieter than normal and he asked Johnsey how was he and Johnsey felt that old painful hardness in his throat the very same as if there was a stone in there, dry and unmoving, blocking the words from coming out, and Himself was still talking and he was telling Johnsey how it was a fright altogether the way they weren't being left in to see him on account of there was police here to beat the band and you wouldn't see a squad from one end of the year to the next besides Jim Gildea in his auld crock of a Renault van and where was this lot when poor Paddy Rourke was getting bate up? And you yourself nearly killed stone dead below in the middle of the village? And now it seemed they was all in the one place together and they all to a man had the same sort of an auld notion that he was up to devilment inside in the house with Jackie's shotgun and did you ever hear the bate of it? Lord God. And Himself laughed and it was a hoarse and whispery thing and maybe not really a laugh at all.

And Johnsey pressed the red button on the phone and it said *call ended* and he could breathe again.

He sat on the easy chair on the far side of the fireplace from the yard window with Daddy's Winchester cradled in his lap like a man might cradle a small child and his left hand lay on top of his right hand on top of the butt and the barrels rested in the crook of his left arm and it was a kind of a comforting thing to be sitting there with that cold weight on him and it was fine and dark at that end of the room where the weak winter light never reached and he wondered what would it be like to pull the soft darkness around him like a blanket and disappear into it.

★　★　★

It had been only a bare few minutes after Dermot McDermott had copped on that there was a gun pointing at his forehead and nearly fell backwards onto his arse with the fright and run

241

off across towards the haggard wall that the lad with the bullhorn had showed up, and lights were flickering, blue and white and orange, and he felt a kind of a pride that he had known to keep himself towards the back of the kitchen where no one would really be able to see him if he kept still enough, but in such a way that he'd be able to squint out now and again to see could he see the Unthanks or the Penroses or Aunty Theresa, who'd no doubt be shaking her head in disbelief at the show he was making of them all, or poor Nonie who'd be clinging on to Frank in fear and confusion, or any face he might know, but there was nothing and nobody to be seen now when he lifted his head but still and all he could feel the weight of them outside the gate and behind the wall, and the mass of them and the density of them, like all things in the universe had, according to that auld science teacher, except the thoughts inside in your head, but that was dead wrong, anyway, because all the minds of them people outside the gate and behind the wall were trained on him now and he could feel the heaviness of their thoughts on him and it was pounding on his head, the pain of the weight of it all.

He imagined Dermot McDermott rubbing his grabbing hands together across the haggard and beyond the trees and over the far side of the river field and laughing with his people about the mad lunatic over beyond and he playing inside in the kitchen with his father's gun, and then going off licking to Jim Gildea below, delighted to be blackening the bad yoke who wouldn't hand over his land. But Johnsey knew he'd shited himself when he'd seen the two black eyes staring at him, with nothing but death inside in them, and that was all that mattered.

★ ★ ★

The heedless clock tick-tocked away for itself, minding nothing only its own maddening business. He sat up a bit in the chair, slowly, slowly, and raised his head and squinted his eyes again and he knew there was still more out there, the lad with the bullhorn was there the whole time and he pouring the odd few grinding, buzzing words into it for himself, and fellas in dark-blue helmets with little stubby guns like toys were chancing the odd dart across the gateway, holding big huge screens like shields beside themselves while they scuttled. Shields, imagine! Did they think he was going to start firing arrows at them? He'd have to go out and clear them to hell. They had the wrong end of the stick got altogether. He was some show! As if he wasn't enough of a show already, in all fairness.

The mobile phone screamed again. He jumped and the gun-butt bucked in his lap and the barrels went from the crook of his arm to the bend of his shoulder blade almost of their own accord, as if they had taken fright and were looking to him for comfort.

When his heart had settled a bit he reached across to the edge of the table for the blasted phone and it was all he could do to press the little green button with his auld awkward thumb and it was Himself again, and he was all talk now, the very same way he'd be on a rainy lunchtime inside in the bakery, and he was asking Johnsey to know how was he now and would he put away that auld gun before he did himself an injury and come away out in the name of God and go easy now, go easy, and they'd see about a bit of lamb for the dinner and Herself was there alongside him still and she was up to ninety worrying about him and she'd gave the whole morning making tarts with the last of the apples they'd collected only a few weeks ago, remember? And he had the finest of cream whipped and all and left in a bowl inside in the fridge, all ready to go for the afters.

Johnsey listened away and he closed his eyes so that he could picture Himself more clearly and when the flow of words softened and slowed he asked to know what had happened to Mumbly Dave.

Dave? Oh Lord, Dave is the solid finest so he is, thanks be to God, that Minnie Wiley ran with a half a story as usual! Don't you know the way the mouths around here work? He slid on that auld bad bend above and he got trapped inside in his car and the brigade had to take the roof off of it to get him out and sure I think half the time they do be only doing that for show, as much as to say Hey lookit, everyone, aren't we the fine boys with our big expensive cutting machine and our jaws of life, and if it was years ago when common sense trumped all, that car would have been righted by three or four strong men and dragged out by a tractor and drove away the finest and the driver gave a bandage and a brandy. But now the minute an ambulance is seen or a siren even heard the worst is presumed and the likes of that Minnie the Mouth do be off with tall tales made taller with each telling. Dave will come round and be up out of that hospital bed in no time and the two of ye will be palling around again and this auld craic will all blow over and be forgot, wait till you see. Like the winds of last winter, Johnsey, love.

Love.

And Johnsey heard a quaver in Himself's voice and saw in spite of himself a picture in his head of a man like one of them men Daddy used talk about that would lie about a beast's provenance beyond at the mart and put wrong numbers on tags and try to sell disease on to another man's herd and the man in the picture had a forked tongue like a snake's because that's the way Daddy would describe a man like that and wasn't it a fright to God how things was gone to be such a way that Johnsey could even imagine Jimmy Unthank to be one of them men?

All talk is lies in a way. Only the doing of a thing can make it true. All words are lies unless the thing spoke about can be set before a person and seen and touched. Things said on mobile telephones and wrote down in ink on paper to be read by all and sundry can't be given any credence any more, nor could they ever. Was it only he could see that? What hope had the world if that was true?

And then Himself was talking again and his

voice was lower and the words were coming at a pace that put him in mind of a tear making its slow way down a person's face the way he'd seen the one on Himself's face do as he stood holding on to the edge of Daddy's coffin that day long ago or the one last night on Mumbly Dave's face, and someone was whispering behind him or beside him and Himself was saying No matter what anyone said or says ever in the future, myself and Herself only ever wanted what was the best for you, for we love you the very same as if you were our own child.

And Johnsey lowered his head and his hand let go of that auld mobile phone and went down to the heavy wood of the butt of Daddy's gun and he chanced a look up from his seat on the easy chair and he saw no one in the gateway but he felt them all there, building up and up, waiting to explode in on top of him, like the water behind that mighty dam the young Dutch boy tried to hold back with his finger, and he wondered was it a true thing that a heart could feel heavy or was that another of them auld sayings where the words don't mean what you might at first think.

The mobile buzzed again from the floor and his breath rushed from him and he picked it up and flung it towards the hearth and it bounced into the grate where it hopped around like a thing propelled by magic and finally came apart and lay in bits in there among the cold ashes.

And that was the end of auld talk on telephones, for good and glory.

★　★　★

When Johnsey got to the front door and opened it, he heard a roaring wind. But there was no stir out of the trees beyond the haggard. It was the sound of his blood, rushing around his body. He'd want to go handy or his heart would burst. He still couldn't make out what your man was saying. Something about using force and then crackle, roar, crackle, roar, crackle. He was badly stuck for a new bullhorn, that fella.

★   ★   ★

Paddy said duck shot never killed nobody, it'd only blister lads. No harm now to give these boys a fright and they'd know then to go on away and leave him alone to hell. The bullhorn lad was gone quare now altogether around the corner of the wall, roaring and screaming out of him, but none of them words made any sense. He was an awful yahoo, that lad. He tucked the butt into his shoulder again. Lord, it fit lovely all the same. They'd get a fright now and they'd all feck off with the help of God. He took one step forward and aimed at the cold blue sky and

★   ★   ★

That's the thing about December: it goes by you in a flash. If you just close your eyes, it's gone. And it's like you were never there.

Acknowledgments

Thanks: To Antony Farrell, Sarah Davis-Goff, Daniel Caffrey, Fiona Dunne, Kitty Lyddon and everyone at The Lilliput Press; to Eoin McHugh, Brian Langan, Larry Finlay, Bill Scott-Kerr, Kate Green, Elspeth Dougall and everyone at Doubleday Ireland and Transworld UK; to Marianne Gunn O'Connor; to Helen Gleed O'Connor, Declan Heeney, Simon Hess and the team at Gill Hess; to Jennifer Johnston, John Boyne and all the writers I've met who have shown such kindness and generosity; to my wonderful parents, Anne and Donie Ryan, for everything; to my sister Mary, who believed in me long before I did; to John, Lindsey, Christopher, Daniel and all my family, for their constant love and support; to Thomas and Lucy, the lights of my life; and to Anne Marie, my beautiful wife, without whom I wouldn't have written a single word.